THE OC

THE SUMMER of SUMMER

The SUMMER of SUMMER

by Cory Martin

SCHOLASTIC INC.
New York Toronto London Auckland Sydney
Mexico City New Delhi Hong Kong Buenos Aires

ISBN 0-439-69633-X

Published by Scholastic Inc.

12 11 10 9 8 7 6 5 4 3 2 1 5 6 7 8 9 10/0

Designed by Louise Bova
Printed in the U.S.A.
First printing, June 2005

1

The air was hot. The sun beat down on the golden beaches where salty waves lapped at the shore. Tanned surfers weaved in and out of the water, their buff bodies working against the tides. Summer had officially begun in Newport.

Summer Roberts and Marissa Cooper lay on the beach soaking up the first rays of the season. Summer's long brown hair blew in the late morning breeze as her soft skin slowly turned golden brown. She looked over at her friend and smiled. It was the first week of summer, school was out, and the drama of their lives seemed to melt away in the heat. This is the life, Summer thought as Marissa opened her eyes and looked up at her.

"What's up?" Marissa asked, propping herself up on her forearm.

"Just thinking," Summer replied. "This is like our first official day of summer. You. Me. The beach. Surfers in the water. It's our ritual."

"Yeah," Marissa said flatly. "Another exciting summer in Newport."

"Coop, come on. It can't be that bad. At least we didn't get ditched this year. Cohen and Ryan are still here."

"True," Marissa answered. "But that doesn't mean it's going to be different."

"You never know. Wait, you didn't —" Summer reached for Marissa's bottled water and took a sip.

"What are you doing?" Marissa asked defensively.

Summer swallowed. "Just checking. Didn't want a repeat of last summer."

"Funny." Marissa smiled, then took her water back and placed it to her lips, downing most of it.

In the past, Marissa had had a habit of drinking when things got rough, and Summer always worried about her friend. Whenever Marissa began making anti-Newport comments, Summer liked to check her drinks because that was how it began. Marissa would get depressed and then she'd start sneaking alcohol, trying to drink her problems away. The summer before last, Marissa would get so drunk that Summer and their other friends often had to carry her to her room. Then there was the infamous trip to Tijuana where Marissa downed so much tequila and so many painkillers that she'd had to be airlifted to a hospital. That had served as a wake-up call and during the next year, Summer had noticed that Marissa had tried to back off the drinking. But then last summer, Ryan, Marissa's boyfriend, had gone back to Chino to be with his ex-girlfriend who might or might not have been carrying his child, and Marissa had slid back into her old habits. She'd spent most of her time inebriated and hazy. Sipping vodka and lemonade while she lay by the pool.

Summer thought about that summer and felt a tinge of guilt. She had sort of abandoned her friend when Cohen disappeared and she met Zach, her boyfriend for most of the year. But this summer was going to be different, she'd promised herself. She was going to keep an eye on her friend and no way would she abandon her for any guy.

"Shit," Summer exclaimed, a thought popping into her head. Something that would disrupt all her carefully laid plans.

"What?" Marissa asked.

"You're right. This summer just might suck after all."

"That was just me being me. Don't get so down," Marissa said, trying to be upbeat.

"No. I'm serious. I just remembered. The step-monster. She told us last week at some family dinner thing she made us go to. We're going on vacation."

Summer looked at her friend for sympathy, but she didn't get it.

"So. What's so bad about that? Unless she's like my mom and she's bribing you because she's sleeping with your boyfriend." Marissa laughed.

"Coop! That's messed up," Summer exclaimed, playfully hitting Marissa's shoulder.

"Welcome to my family," Marissa said as she lay back down and shut her eyes.

"No thanks, I don't even want to go into that mess. No offense," Summer said, sitting up.

"None taken."

"No. We're going to Seascape," Summer explained.

"It's nice. Caleb took us there for brunch once when my mom was trying to make us seem like one big happy family," Marissa said as she flipped over and let the sun warm the smooth skin of her stomach.

"Yeah. But it's in Laguna. Ten miles from here," Summer said, trying to justify her discontent.

"So?" Marissa asked, still showing no sympathy.

"*So*? Ewww. It's like MTV generic. At least last year, when whatever ailment the monster had kept us from going far, we got to go to the Four Seasons. And Fashion Island was a short walk across the parking lot."

"True," Marissa agreed.

"And I even tried to see if you could come, but the stepmonster's on new meds. Apparently she can travel now, and she wants this to be a 'family' vacation . . . whatever *that* means."

"Do you ever think we'll have normal families one day?" Marissa asked.

"You mean like a normal family that takes a real vacation to a cool, exotic place and meets interesting people?" Summer asked. Marissa nodded. Summer thought for a second, then replied, "Look at us. We spend our days on the beach soaking up sun, complaining about our lives. Of course not. We've got to be punished somehow."

"Never thought about it like that."

"Me neither. Apparently when you have a crazy stepmother these sorts of things come to you," Summer said.

"Yeah. Must only work with stepparents. 'Cause I've got the crazy mother, and nothing good's come of that." Marissa laughed.

Summer smiled and lay back down on her towel. The sun was directly overhead now. She was glad that summer had arrived and school was out, but she really was dreading this "family" vacation. She and her father were close. He adored her and she him, but somehow when her stepmother was around, the bond between them weakened. It was as if the meds seeped into all their lives and instead of making life easier they poisoned it. For the monster, the meds were a cure for whatever phobia, mental illness, or just plain disarray she was suffering from that month. But for Summer they only made things good for a week or so, while her stepmother was first experiencing the numbing effects, then as she adjusted, the paranoia would return, and Summer's life would be back to where it started. Then it was just easier for Summer to avoid her stepmother and try to get by on her own.

"I really wish you could come," Summer said as-she picked up a bottle of suntan lotion and squeezed a bit onto her legs. "Need some?" she asked, holding out the bottle.

Marissa opened her hand and Summer squeezed some lotion into it, which Marissa rubbed into her prominent collarbones. "Yeah, I know. But it's not like it's that far away. I could always come visit."

"True. But how much fun would it have been to spend the days at the pool and the afternoons in the spa? We could've gotten every treatment imagi nable. Come back to Newport with a fresh new glow."

"Have you told Seth yet?" Marissa asked as she wiped her hands on her towel.

Summer paused. She hadn't told him. If she didn't tell him, would that be revenge? Payback for last summer when he just left her a note and took off. Summer thought for a second. That would be kind of nice. Make him worry for a week. Just leave him a note. A truncated good-bye. But then she remembered how crushed she had been and she couldn't do that to anyone, even if he deserved it. "No. I guess I should tell him."

Marissa smiled. *Probably.*

"Are we still meeting them at the Bait Shop tonight?"

"I think so."

"I'll tell him then. Hey, Coop, what was it like?" Marissa turned her head toward Summer and put up her hand to block the sun from her eyes. *What?* "You know. Having a girlfriend."

"I don't know, same as having a boyfriend," Marissa answered nonchalantly.

"Really?" Summer asked in a skeptical voice. They had talked about Marissa's relationship with Alex, the Bait Shop manager, who happened to be a girl, but they had never really talked about the implications. "*So*, you had the usual petty fights? The jealousy. The insecurities . . . The love?" Summer asked, finally getting to her real question.

Marissa hesitated before answering. "I wouldn't go that far. But she made me see a part of myself I'd never seen."

"I guess a good boyfriend, or girlfriend, does that," Summer said, thinking about her own past, about Zach and Seth.

"Yeah, I guess."

Summer wondered if Marissa still had feelings for her ex. If she missed her. While it was hard for her to fully understand the idea of what Marissa had gone through, because she had never had those kinds of feelings, she knew how happy Alex had made Marissa, and she found that sweet. She knew what it was like to fall for someone, to have your whole world revolve around just one person. To be happy and content, and maybe, just maybe, on the brink of love. And she believed that it didn't matter who that person was, she just knew that happiness was hard to come by.

"You know, you dated Seth's ex. Does that mean one day you're going to date me?" Summer asked with a smile. Trying to lighten the mood, which had gotten suddenly somber.

"You're not really my type." Marissa laughed.

"Hey!" Summer giggled, trying to sound hurt.

The girls laughed, sitting up on their towels to look out at the waves pounding on the shore.

"See, this summer might not be so bad after all."

"Yeah. At least I don't have to go to Seascape with my stepmother. It'll be great."

"Ugh. Don't remind me," Summer sighed.

"When do you leave?"

"Tomorrow."

"So tonight's your first and last night of summer for now?"

"You could say that," Summer said with disappointment.

"We'll just have to make the best of it. . . ."

Summer nodded as she watched one really hot surfer come out of the water, her lips slowly moving into a smile at the sight of him. "Yeah, we will."

When Summer got home that afternoon, she started packing for the week in Laguna. She put her two Louis Vuitton suitcases on top of her bed and stared at them. It was as if the empty suitcases were mocking her, telling her how horrible this vacation was going to be—empty and boring. Summer sighed and sank onto the bed. Princess Sparkles looked up at her from her nightstand.

"What?" Summer asked the horse. "Want to go in my place?"

The horse said nothing. Summer sighed again and brushed the horse's mane. What was she going to do? This was going to be torture. There was nothing to do in Laguna. If they didn't get to go to Cannes or Fiji or somewhere else exotic and expensive, why couldn't they just go to the Four Seasons again? At least there she would feel at home. Laguna was like worlds away.

Summer put Princess Sparkles back on the nightstand and went to her closet. She better start packing; the sooner she sealed her bags, the sooner they could leave and the sooner this disaster would be over and she could get back to her life.

She sifted through her closet, looking for the perfect outfits to take with her. She might as well look good, even if the vacation was going to suck. As she pulled dress after dress out of her closet and placed them in the suitcases, Summer thought about how much better it would be if she were going somewhere new. She could dress in amazing outfits, meet exotic new people, and gorgeous men with foreign accents would fall in love with her . . . but not in Laguna.

As Summer pulled a few bikinis from her dresser and placed them in her suitcase, there was a knock at the door.

"I'm packing. Naked," she said, trying to avoid any more pep talks from her dad or stepmother about how great this vacation was going to be.

"Do you do everything naked?" a voice asked from the other side of the door. It wasn't her father. It was Seth, her sometimes boyfriend and sometimes friend.

She opened the door. "Only in your dreams, Cohen."

"It's true. You did look pretty good last night," he joked, standing in the doorway.

Summer playfully slapped him. "Don't even try to replay that in your mind."

"Your stepmom seems pretty cheerful today."

"A thousand new meds," Summer answered as she let Seth inside her room. Seth started to laugh but stopped himself as soon as he saw the giant suitcases sprawled out on the bed.

"Going somewhere?" he asked.

Summer looked at the bags, then back at Seth. Right. She stepped in front of him and put out her arms, trying to hide the suitcases. "Um, actually . . ." she began, then decided to really mess with him. "I was trying to leave before you noticed. Maybe I'd leave you a note. Try and call you once or twice, but that's about it."

"Funny," Seth started. "So you packed all your bags just to make a witty comment. I'm impressed. Farther than I'd ever take it, but good."

Summer smiled mischievously at him, but Seth missed it. He was too wrapped up in himself.

He sat on the bed and picked up Princess Sparkles. "Are you going on this imaginary trip, too?" he asked the horse. "Maybe Captain Oats can join you."

Summer reached out for Princess Sparkles and put her in the suitcase on top of her swimsuits. "Actually, she is. And Captain Oats can maybe come; that's up to Princess Sparkles. She may want to meet some new horses on this vacation."

"Really? And where are you two going?"

"Seascape."

"In Laguna? That's like ten miles away. What were you going to do, leave me a note, then spy on me every night?"

"No. It's the meds," Summer tried to explain.

"You're on them, too?"

"No. Ass. I'm not on meds. The stepmonster has a new outlook on life. She wants us to go on a family vacation and bond. It's going to be hell. Want to come visit?"

"Is your dad going?"

"Family vacation sort of implies yes."

"Um, then no thanks. The two of us don't really—"

"Right. The vim and the vigor. And what was it? Ice Man?" Summer laughed, recalling the one time Seth had met her father. It was brunch at the yacht club and Seth had turned into a bumbling idiot. Summer had been completely embarrassed and they'd almost broken up, but they hadn't and she'd thought things would be fine. Then, just a few weeks later, Seth had left her with a stupid note. How had she ended up back with him anyways? Because he was Cohen and he had some way of charming her . . .

"Hey. He melts things," Seth said in defense of Ice Man.

"I'm going to melt you if you don't get out of my way," Summer said. "If I don't finish packing now I can't meet you guys later."

But Seth didn't move. She could see the wheels turning in his head. "What now, Cohen?"

"How about I help you?"

"Fine," Summer said as she reached into her underwear drawer and started pulling out handfuls of bras and panties. "Put these in there," she finished as she threw them at Seth.

Seth held out his hands and caught the pile of undergarments. But as he put them in the suitcase he started inspecting each piece. "I thought you were going to Laguna, not Fritz's."

"Fritz's?"

"The finest strip club in Anaheim," Seth answered as if he knew. Summer glared at him as she pulled her bra out of his hand and placed it in the suitcase. "Luke told me about it," he admitted. Summer glared again. "It was a long summer."

"Yeah. I remember. Now are you going to help me or not?"

"If you promise to put this away," Seth said as he held up a lacy bra. "And replace it with something more like this," he finished as he picked up a sports bra with full coverage.

"Fine," she said as she grabbed both the bras and put them in her bag.

"I said replace, not put them both in there. Who are you going to wear those for anyways?"

"No one, Cohen. I'm going to Seascape. It's old, crusty, and—"

"Full of rich men," Seth finished, a tinge of nervousness in his voice.

Summer thought for a moment. Seth had a point. "You're right. I'm not making any promises," she said, trying to get a rise out of him. They had a habit of doing that to each other, pushing each other's buttons, seeing how far they could go.

Seth looked down at the suitcases. His mind racing. Summer continued to pack. Ignoring him.

"I'm taking her as collateral," Seth said as he picked up Princess Sparkles from the suitcase. "She can stay with Captain Oats for the week. You return in one piece, so does Princess Sparkles."

Summer stopped what she was doing and shook her head in dismay. "What do you think I'm going to do? It's Laguna, Seth. Not a third-world country."

"I'm just taking precautions, Summer."

"Fine," Summer said as she reached for Seth's hand and ushered him to the door. "Take her with you, but I've got to finish this. I'll see you later."

And as Summer shut the door on Seth, she thought about how crazy he was, and how she kept coming back to him.

The sound of an acoustic guitar and the beat of drums echoed from the Bait Shop, Newport's all-ages concert venue and nightclub. Marissa, Summer, Seth, and Ryan stood in line on the pier.

Summer was ready to have a good time, when the bouncer suddenly appeared and announced that the club was at capacity for the evening. He couldn't let anyone else in.

"Great," Summer said. "Last night in Newport and we're stuck doing nothing." Then she looked at Seth and Marissa. "Hey, maybe if you two hadn't *both* dated the manager we could pull some strings and get in."

"Hey," Seth started, "don't blame me. Marissa was the last one to date her."

"Okay, you three. Can we not fight and figure out something to do?" Ryan asked before the discussion could escalate.

"I liked you better when you didn't say anything," Summer responded. Ryan smiled at her and laughed.

"PlayStation, anyone?" Seth asked, trying to come up with anything.

Ryan and Marissa looked at each other and shrugged their shoulders. *Why not?*

Summer looked at Seth. Was he serious? But when she got in the car she realized he was.

What a great way to start a vacation! Summer thought as she stared at the television. *I can't wait!*

2

Summer stared out the window of her father's Mercedes as they drove down Pacific Coast Highway toward Laguna. The lush green lawns and mansions of Newport essentially turned into more of the same. To the outside eye, the two cities looked pretty much the same, but to Summer, they were polar opposites. Laguna was full of older retirees, Newport was alive with her life. As her father drove and her stepmom chattered away, Summer wondered if she'd make it through the week. They were barely out of Newport and already she missed her friends and her bed and . . .

Ye-e—e-ah. Her train of thought was interrupted by a sudden shrill yell coming from the passenger seat. Summer shot straight up in her seat, completely startled. The stepmonster was alive. Her window was open and her head was just outside it, the wind blowing in her hair. Summer looked over at the other lane of traffic. Had anyone just seen that? Not a car in sight. Summer sank back into her seat with a sigh of relief. She had been spared a moment of embarrassment. For now, she thought. But as she looked to the front of the car she saw her stepmother reach over and place her hand on her dad's thigh and give it a loving squeeze. *Ewww!*

By the time they arrived at the hotel, Summer couldn't wait to get out of the car. But she'd only been in her room for a few minutes when her stepmom came knocking. She was wearing a sheer beach cover-up, her silicon-enhanced breasts buoyed by her white string bikini. Summer's stomach dropped. Could this get any worse?

"Ready for the pool? I need a Sea Breeze. My Klonopin is wearing off."

Summer just stared at her. Where was her dad? Wasn't he supposed to be spending quality time with his wife? Summer looked down toward their room, but there was no one in sight.

"Neil is making tee times for tomorrow. Put your suit on. He'll meet us later. Come on. I won't bite," the monster said with a mock chomp of her teeth.

Reluctantly, Summer went back into her room and put on her yellow bikini, her favorite because it gave her the sexiest tan lines. If she had to lay by the pool with her stepmom, at least she could get something good out of it.

The pool was surrounded by lush flowers and palm trees. The blue of the water echoed the blue of the sky. The smell of chlorine filled the air.

Summer checked out the rest of the people

around the water. There was no one her age, just screaming kids and geriatrics with a lot of plastic surgery. Even the pool boys were old and boring. *Some vacation this is going to be,* Summer thought. She needed eye candy. At least last summer when she and Marissa spent most of their time around Marissa's pool, they had DJ, the yard guy, to look at. But now there was nothing.

Summer put her towel on a lounge chair next to the monster, who had already oiled up her skin and ordered a drink from one of the pool boys.

Summer put on her SPF 30 lotion. She didn't want to look forty by the time she was thirty. Especially since thirty was the new twenty. And after seeing all the pain her stepmom went through just to have perfect skin, she wasn't really ready to fry. She just wanted a nice golden glow.

"Is there anything else I can get you, Ms. Roberts?" Summer looked over at the pool boy who was talking to the monster. *Run now before she attacks.* Summer wanted to warn the poor guy, but it was too late.

Before she could be forced to listen to any strange demands, Summer put the earphones to her iPod in her ears and turned on Lynn Grabhorn's *Excuse Me, Your Life Is Waiting.* This place was already bringing her down and she needed to attract some positive energy. She needed to start vibrating at a high frequency so that she could find someone else vibrating at a similar frequency.

Summer lay back and let the sun relax every muscle in her body. With her iPod turned up high, she could drown out all the distraction and embarrassment. Maybe things weren't so bad after all. . . .

After an hour, Summer awoke from a nap to find the monster at the edge of the pool talking to a buff older man who appeared to be in charge of the kids' club activities.

"Come here, Sum," the stepmonster yelled when she saw that Summer was awake.

At first Summer tried to pretend that she hadn't heard her. But eventually the monster started to cause a scene, waving her arms about, and Summer decided to go over before it got worse.

"Oh, good. You heard me," said her stepmom.

"Yeah, you could say that," Summer replied.

"Sum," the monster began, making Summer cringe—she hated when the stepmonster called her that. "This is Gary."

The buff man held out his hand and Summer shook it. "Nice to meet you," she said. "I'm going to go back over and—"

But the stepmonster cut her off. "Wait. Not yet. I told Gary how you missed your friends and I thought maybe you could join the kids' club tomorrow. Hang out with them. What do you think?"

"I think I'm too old. But thanks anyway," Summer answered quickly, going back to her chair and gathering her stuff.

This really was the worst vacation ever. Not only was she in Laguna, only ten miles from home, but now her stepmother wanted her to play with little kids. As if she still wanted to play. Whatever that meant.

Back in her suite, Summer dialed Marissa's cell phone and was relieved when her friend picked up after just two rings.

"Sanity!" Summer exclaimed without even saying hello.

"That bad?" Marissa asked.

"You have no idea," Summer said as she fell back onto the giant bed. "Give me some good gossip. Tell me something exciting. I don't even want to think about my day, let alone talk about it."

"Seth misses you."

"What? Why?" Summer asked, shocked.

"He came over today."

"Really? Has he ever come over to your place before? Alone?"

"Yeah. Once. Beginning of last year. He missed you. It was after he found out about you and Zach and he realized he couldn't have you back."

"Oh," Summer said, remembering the Kick-off Carnival at the beginning of the school year when Seth had once again tried to declare his love for her but she had turned to Zach instead. Seth had had his chance. He'd had her and he'd left. It was then that she'd realized that Seth only loved the chase. Whenever she was available, he tired of her, but when she was unavailable or like now, not in sight, he became obsessed with her. "That's typical Cohen," she said. Then she had another thought.

"Oh, no. He didn't come to you to ask what he could do to show his love for me?"

"Actually, he did. I told him you liked guys in clown suits to show up at your door and serenade you with sweet songs."

"I'm scared of clowns," Summer said, now worried that someone really was going to show up at her door and start singing to her.

"I know." Marissa laughed. "I was joking. I told him that you'd call him later. That he should just be happy with a phone call. He didn't need a grand gesture."

"That's why you're my best friend. I love you."

"Love you, too. Now go call him before he shows up here again and starts harassing me."

"Thanks, Coop," Summer finished as she hung up the phone.

She sat up and dialed Seth. When he picked up he seemed in a panic. "Summer, you're alive!"

"Cohen, I've only been gone for a few hours."

"I know, but I need you to check in. Every hour. Don't worry, I make Ryan do it, too, when he goes away. Have you met any rich men yet?"

"Seth. Calm down. No, I haven't met any rich men. And no I am not going to call you every hour on the hour. That's ridiculous."

"How about every other hour?"

"Cohen!" Summer exclaimed.

"Okay, fine. Once every three hours. That's my final offer. Take it or leave it."

"I'll agree on one term."

"What's that?"

"That you come rescue me."

"Oh. A real superhero adventure. That I can do."

"Thank god," Summer sighed.

"But not tonight. I promised Ryan I'd take him to the Imax theater. We've been trying to go for years. Our schedules finally match up and—"

"You suck," Summer said before Seth could finish. She wanted him to come rescue her now. She knew that her dad and the monster would be back soon, and they'd want to go to dinner. She had to be gone by then.

"How about tomorrow? I'm supposed to go sailing with some of the guys from the yacht club. We were going to go to Emerald Bay, but we could swing by Seascape and I'll take the dinghy into shore to get you."

"What time?" Summer asked.

"Be on the beach at one, and don't meet any rich guys."

"I don't think you have to worry," Summer said as she remembered all the young kids and the plasticized geriatrics who were at the pool earlier in the day. "I'll see you tomorrow."

That night, Summer barely made it through a grueling dinner with her dad and the stepmonster. The only thing that kept her going was the knowledge that tomorrow Seth would come and rescue her. All she had to do was make it through the night.

But now as they sat at the table waiting for

dessert to arrive, Summer started to worry that she just might not make it after all.

"Do you hear that?" the monster asked. Summer and her dad both shook their heads. "The music. From the ballroom. We have to dance," the monster said.

Summer looked to her father. She wanted him to say no. That they didn't have to dance. That they were done being a family for the evening, but instead he said okay. And after the bill had been settled, the monster insisted on leading them to the ballroom, where music was playing softly and happy old couples were dancing all around.

Maybe I can dance with Dad, Summer thought. But when she went to reach for her father's hand, the stepmonster had beaten her to it.

Summer found a leather club chair in the corner of the room and took a seat. She was alone and bored. It was only eight o'clock and already she longed for bed. The sooner she went to sleep, the sooner it would be tomorrow, and she could wake up and find Seth.

But for now, she was stuck here in this ballroom with the monster, her dad, and about twenty old couples. It reminded her of the cotillion where she had made her debut into Newport society. Seth was supposed to be her date, but at the time, she couldn't stand him and when she'd finally gotten rid of him, she found herself without a date. But when she tried to get Seth back as her date, he'd already found someone new. Anna. The two girls had eventually become friends, and Summer had to admit that without Anna she would never have realized that she loved Seth. After Anna moved back to Pittsburgh, Summer hadn't really heard from her, but now she wondered what Anna was doing at that exact moment. Her mind concocted story after story about how much better the lives of everyone she knew were than hers right now.

But just as she decided she'd had enough of feeling sorry for herself and was heading out of the ballroom, someone stopped her.

"Leaving so soon?" a voice asked. Summer looked up and saw a guy her age.

She just smiled and tried to walk away, but the boy wasn't giving up. He kept blocking her path.

"I have to go. Do you mind?" Summer snapped.

"What's the rush? Hot date? We're the only ones our age here."

"There is no we. And I'm tired," Summer said as she tried to squeeze by. But he stopped her once more.

"Where you from?" the boy asked.

"You first," Summer said, not wanting to admit that she had gone on vacation ten miles from her house.

"Chicago."

"The middle of the flyover zone? Not interested," she said and again she tried to move past him.

"Who said anything about being interested? I was just looking for a friend."

"I've got enough friends, but thanks," Summer said and this time she managed to squeeze by him.

As she made her way to the door, the boy yelled after her, "See you around."

But Summer didn't care. She didn't need some random friend from the middle of nowhere. She had Seth and she'd see him tomorrow.

3

That night, Seth and Ryan drove around Newport looking for something to do. As they stopped at the traffic light before Newport Shores, Seth turned to Ryan.

"Hey, buddy. This is our first official summer. I mean, there was that brief time when you first moved in, but that was the end of the summer. You haven't been able to enjoy the full Newport experience. I think we should officially declare this the summer of Seth and Ryan."

"Okay," Ryan said as he tugged at his seat belt to make sure it was secure. He never knew with Seth and his plans. "So what does that entail exactly?"

"The usual. Balboa bars. Rides on the ferry. Nights in the fun zone. Surfing. Picking up hotties on the beach. Tossing the old pigskin around. Parties. Kegstands."

"Since when do you throw the pigskin and pick up 'hotties'?" Ryan laughed.

"Ryan, how long have I been your brother now?" Seth stepped on the gas as the light turned green.

"Almost two years."

"And you still don't know me? That's sad. Really sad. I almost feel bad for leaving you last summer."

"You left *Summer*. Remember? Not me."

"Oh my god. You're right." Seth slammed on the brakes and took a hard right at Orange. He had to turn around. "Wait, and now she's leaving me. Do you think this is payback?"

"Seth, she's on vacation for a week. In Laguna. She didn't move to Iowa," Ryan replied, trying to calm Seth. He looked out the window at the burger joint they were parked next to.

"I know. That's my point. Most accidents happen within a mile of home."

"You've lost it."

"We're going to Marissa's," Seth said as he got back on the highway and headed south toward Marissa's house.

"Why?"

"I have to talk to her. Ugh. I can't believe I blew off Summer for an Imax movie," Seth sighed as he sped along the way.

"I thought you and I were bonding. What happened to the summer of Seth and Ryan?"

"That's going to have to wait. It's now the summer of Summer," Seth said as he thought about his phone call with her earlier in the evening. How could he have blown her off? She'd probably already met someone new and forgotten about him. That's what vacations did. Especially when you were running away. This was turning into the worst summer ever, Seth thought.

As Seth pulled into Marissa's driveway, he noticed that her bedroom light was still on. Perfect.

He looked at Ryan, who seemed a bit nervous.

"Don't worry, buddy. She's probably expecting me."

Ryan just nodded. *Sure.*

Seth didn't want to risk waking Marissa's mom, so he called Marissa's cell phone and told her that he and Ryan were waiting downstairs.

When Marissa appeared at the door, Ryan immediately began to apologize. "Don't blame me. It's all him. He's on a weird kick right now."

Marissa nodded. She already knew. Then she looked at Seth. *What now?*

"It's Summer."

"She called you, right?" Marissa asked. Seth nodded. "Well, then what's the problem?"

"She said she'd call every three hours."

"She agreed to that?"

"Well, not exactly. But still. I ditched her tonight and now she's probably with some other guy and that's the end of there ever being a Seth and Summer, if you know what I mean."

"I told you he was crazy," Ryan chimed in, then took a step back before Seth could hit him.

"Seth," Marissa began as Seth continued to pace back and forth in panicked Seth mode. "What did you say to her on the phone? How did you leave things?"

"I told her I'd pick her up tomorrow at one."

"So meet her at one. She'll be there. Stop worrying. There's no other guy."

But Seth couldn't leave things at that. "See, Ryan, even Marissa is thinking about the other guy. I need to do something big." Seth began walking away. "Let's go. We got some planning to do," he added, grabbing Ryan's arm.

"Just *show up,* Cohen. Don't leave her like you did last summer," Marissa called after them.

Seth raised his arm in a sign of thanks, then hopped in the car and sped along his way. He had a lot of planning to do before tomorrow. This had to be the best sailing trip ever if he was going to win Summer back.

4

After a morning of spa treatments with the step-monster, Summer made her way through the grounds of the resort to a private beach. The sun was shining, and waves calmly lapped at the shore. It was perfect sailing weather.

Summer put her towel down on the sand and took a seat. Seth would be here soon and she wanted to look calm and collected, not totally desperate to be rescued. The beach was fairly empty and she was enjoying the solitude. There were no screaming kids, no monster, and no old women with fake skin.

But just as Summer was starting to get comfortable and enjoy the solitude, a voice spoke from behind her. "Hey, I know you."

It wasn't Seth and it wasn't her dad. Summer got a sinking feeling in her stomach. Was it who she thought it was? She turned around. Yes. It was the boy from last night. The one from Chicago. The one she totally blew off.

"Told you I'd see you around," he said.

"Guess you were right," Summer replied as she flipped her hair away from her face.

"So. Find anyone our age to hang out with lately?" He asked as he sat down next to her on her towel.

Summer scooted away a little.

"Actually, I'm waiting for my boyfriend. He's sailing here," she said quickly.

"Wow, you must be some girl to get a boy to sail around the world for you."

"What are you talking about?"

"Well, I figured since Chicago wasn't really your thing you must be from somewhere exotic. The French Riviera was my first guess, but I'm willing to take a bet on the Greek Isles as well."

Summer was taken aback for a second. For someone from the flyover zone, he was pretty quick with the comebacks.

"Neither. But good try," Summer replied as she looked out at the sea. Where was Seth?

"I see. A girl of mystery. Well, I'll leave you to wait for your boyfriend, but if you get bored or the trip around the world takes longer than expected, I'll be up in the garden reading. No pressure. Just if you want to hang out or something. You know, ditch these geriatrics."

Summer smiled and politely said, "Thanks, but he'll be here."

The boy stood up and headed back to the resort. Summer watched him walk away. For someone who was kind of annoying, he was actually pretty cute. She turned back to face the open ocean, forcing those thoughts out of her head. Seth was on his way to rescue her; she did *not* need to be checking out other guys.

Summer lay back on her towel and waited.

. . . And waited . . .

. . . And waited . . .

She looked at her watch. One forty-five. Where was Seth?

The sea was empty. Calm. Not a boat in sight.

Was she being ditched? Was Seth doing it again? Was he trying to start this summer the same way he had started the last? Leaving her. Alone. Stranded in Laguna.

Summer forced herself to relax. If Seth said he would come at one then he would be here — eventually. And so she continued to wait. . . .

Forty minutes later, Seth still hadn't shown.

She pulled out her phone and tried his cell, but it went straight to voice mail.

That's it, Summer thought, if Cohen hadn't been in a car accident or something she was going to kill him.

Summer picked up her towel and headed back to the resort.

As she walked up the beach she tried to call Marissa and tell her what an ass Cohen was, but Marissa wasn't answering her phone, either. *Where was everyone?* She was stranded in the middle of Laguna and none of her friends were answering their phones. Too bad Ryan didn't have a cell, so she could try him, too. Instead she sent a text message to Marissa: COHEN SUCKS! AGAIN!

After the message went through, Summer turned off her phone. As she walked up the stairs from the beach, she passed by the garden. She paused for a second. She could see the Midwestern boy sitting on a bench, reading. She looked back at the ocean behind her. Still empty. She hesitated for a moment and decided. She was ten miles from home and the familiarity of Newport and she was all alone. Seth had ditched her and there was no one else to talk to. She had nothing to lose.

Summer walked through the garden and approached his bench with a smile. "Can I sit here?" she asked. The boy nodded and scooted to his right to make room for her. Summer sat down, then thought about what to say. . . .

"Uh, thanks," Summer finally muttered as she got comfortable on the bench.

"No problem," the boy answered as he continued to stare at his book. *Great,* Summer thought, *now he was playing the mysterious type.* She would have to start the conversation.

"What are you reading?" she asked.

"*The Lost Legends of New Jersey*. Have you read it?"

Summer shook her head. "No."

"You should."

"Yeah," Summer said. This was harder than she expected.

The boy went back to reading. Obviously any conversation would have to come from her.

"I'm Summer," she said, holding out her hand. He took her hand and gently shook it.

"Losing the mystery, huh? Why the sudden change of heart?"

Summer sat for a minute, formulating a response. She didn't want to admit that she'd been ditched. "Let's just say the trip around the world's taking longer than eighty days."

"Figured. I'm Eric," he said as he finally let go of her hand. "Nice to meet you."

Summer smiled at him. He really was kind of cute.

"So, Summer, what brings you around the world to Seascape?"

Summer paused for a second. Would she tell him that she only lived a short distance away? No. She had a better idea. "My stepmonster forced us to come on a 'family trip.' How about you?"

"I live here."

"You work here?" Summer asked, a slight hint of disappointment in her voice.

"No. You see those villas over there—" Eric pointed to a row of approximately ten large beach houses on the water nearby. "I live there."

"I thought you said you were from Chicago?" Summer asked, totally confused.

"I am. My very own stepmonster forced us here, too. Except she made my dad sell our cabin on

Lake Michigan to buy this place. We've spent the last six summers here."

"Isn't that like an upgrade?" Summer asked, not really clear on why anyone would want to live on a lake if they had the option of living on the ocean.

"To some. Not me," he replied.

Summer looked down at the ground, hoping for conversational inspiration. That was when she noticed his flip-flops. They were completely worn. "So you're one of those hippie types who denounces all material possessions?"

"I wouldn't say that. I just know there's more out there than the Pacific Ocean."

"I know. There's the Atlantic, too. And the Hamptons," Summer said. She knew her geography.

"That's what I thought."

"What?" Summer asked. What had she said?

"Nothing. It's just. You're . . ." Summer looked at him. *What?* "Interesting."

"That's not so bad. Unless you meant that in a bad way?" Summer said, suddenly suspicious.

Eric shook his head no, but she could see on his face that it was more than that.

"You did. Didn't you?" she asked, the panic growing.

"No. You just have a lot to learn. You don't venture much beyond the doors of your French Riviera flat, do you?"

Summer stared at him. What was he talking about?

"Metaphorically, I mean. You don't like to travel much farther than the comforts of your home and your family."

"What are you talking about?" she asked, totally thrown.

"Just asking."

"Fine. I like my home and my family, well, except for the monster, and I like my friends. What's so wrong about that?"

"Nothing. Come on, let's go," Eric said, standing up and placing his book in his back pocket.

"Where?" Summer asked.

"Just trust me."

"I barely know you." She hesitated.

"Yeah, but you sat down next to me. You must have been somewhat curious."

You're right. But Summer didn't say it, just got up and followed Eric through the garden. What did she have to lose? Seth had ditched her. Marissa wasn't answering her phone. And even though Eric was kind of a jerk, he was cute.

Eric led Summer to the villa he had pointed out earlier.

"You're taking me home with you?" she asked as they approached his house.

Eric smiled back at her. "I'm not taking you home. We just had to get these," he said as he pulled open a side garage door and revealed several beach cruiser bikes.

Summer looked down at her short skirt. "We're going on a bike ride?"

Eric nodded, but Summer hesitated and pointed to the short hem of her skirt.

"You have your bathing suit on underneath there, don't you?"

Summer nodded yes.

"Then who cares?"

Summer hesitated, but Eric was right. She did have her bathing suit on and she was comfortable showing that to everyone. So what was the big deal anyways? Well, besides the fact that she and Marissa used to make fun of the girls who rode around Newport in their short skirts. But that was different. Those girls were like going out to dinner, not to the beach. *If Marissa could see me now . . .*

Eric pulled two bikes out of the garage and handed the shorter one to Summer. She placed her beach bag in the front basket and unsteadily mounted the bike. It had been a few years since she had ridden a bike and she got off to a shaky start. But Eric encouraged her to keep pedaling and eventually she got the hang of it.

"Okay, can we leave my driveway now?" he asked.

"Sure," Summer called out as she headed for the street. "Where're we going?"

"Follow me," Eric yelled as he sped up ahead of her and down the road toward the resort entrance.

As they rode, Summer took one last look back at the ocean. The wind had picked up and the solid blue was interrupted by sprays of white; the waves were pounding. Still, there was no boat. She looked down into her bag and saw that her phone was still off. For a moment she contemplated turning it back on. Just in case. But as she looked ahead at Eric, who was riding without hands, flying down the road, laughing, enjoying himself, Summer took it as a sign. The phone would stay off. She was going to give Eric a shot. A shot at becoming her friend.

THE OC

5

"What am I going to tell her? The sail had a hole in it and the wind was dying and all the ropes to the jib were messed up and then we had barnacles on the rudder and it wouldn't steer and just about everything that could go wrong did," Seth rambled to Marissa as he paced about in front of her.

Marissa looked down at the text message she had just received from Summer. COHEN SUCKS! *Seth needed a better excuse.* "Probably not that. Even if all of that's true, it still sounds like the worst lie I've ever heard in my entire life. And coming from the girl who used to sneak booze every night from her parents' liquor cabinet, that's saying a lot."

"How did you get away with all that?"

Marissa just smiled.

"Never mind. The focus is me here. This is selfish Seth needing help. Can you help me?" Seth pleaded.

Marissa nodded as she approached one of the ice cream vendors. Then she turned back to Seth. "I need a Balboa Bar first."

"Fine," Seth said as he paid for the treat.

Marissa took off the wrapper and held the cold ice cream to her mouth.

"What do I do?" Seth begged before Marissa could even take her first bite.

"I don't know. Apologize?" she suggested.

"Well, yeah. But what do I tell her?"

"That the boat got messed up and it was completely out of your control. And wait, how come you didn't just call her?"

"Because by the time I found my phone, which was buried under like a million life jackets, which we had to pull out of the boat in order to scoop out-the water that had practically flooded it . . ." Marissa shook her head in disbelief. "Never mind. Let's just say another thing went wrong. Anyways, by the time I got the phone, she had already tried calling me and when I called back her phone was off."

"Oh," Marissa said. "Then I guess there's only one thing left to do."

"Five dozen roses?"

"No. You have to go there. Find her and apologize in person. If you just leave a message or a note she's going to think you're doing the exact thing you did last summer."

"You're right. Thanks. Did anyone ever tell you you're a genius?"

Marissa smiled as Seth started running down the pier.

"And you have really shiny hair," Seth yelled

as he practically disappeared into the crowds of people.

Marissa laughed to herself as she continued to eat her ice cream. And as she watched Seth fade into oblivion she sent Summer a text message: HE'S ON HIS WAY TO APOLOGIZE!

THE OC

6

After riding for what seemed like hours, Summer and Eric arrived at the heart of Laguna. It was full of shops and restaurants and little boutiques. Summer liked Eric already. This was her kind of scene. She was up for shopping any day.

"I like you already," Summer called to Eric as he pulled into a parking lot with a bike rack.

"Really?" he asked with a sly tone.

"Yeah. This is perfect. So much better than that stuffy resort. I love shopping."

"Um. One thing. We're not going shopping."

"We're not?" Summer asked, disappointed.

"Well, I mean we can look around, but there's some people I want you to meet."

"Already introducing me to your friends? And we haven't even shared our first kiss," Summer said with a smile. She liked messing with Eric. Flirting. Leading him on. Basically, the only way she knew how to relate to guys. When she thought about it, she really didn't even have any guy friends, except for maybe Luke or Ryan, but those were Marissa's boyfriends. The only guy she had ever really been friends with was Seth. But even then there was banter and flirting, even when they were both dating other people.

Summer watched as Eric locked up their bikes, tugging nervously at the hem of her skirt. She was embarrassed that she had even ridden the bike with a skirt on in the first place. But she quickly got over it as Eric grabbed her hand and led her into the little village full of shops.

"Come on," he said as he tugged at her hand. "There's something I want you to try."

Summer looked down at her hand, which was wrapped in Eric's. She thought about pulling away but decided against it. It wasn't as though they were really holding hands; he was just leading the way and she was following. "Okay," she said. "But I only try *on*, not try things. So if this involves clothes, I'm in. Otherwise I'm out."

Eric looked back at her and smiled. "Just follow me," he said as he let go of her hand.

She paused for a minute and looked at her empty palm, then looked back up at Eric, who was already several yards ahead of her. She'd have to follow.

By the time she finally caught up with him, Eric had stopped walking.

"Thanks for waiting," Summer said as she stood next to him. "What's the rush?"

"Just the best tacos ever," Eric exclaimed.

Summer looked up at the little restaurant sign they were standing under. CHANO'S TACOS.

Eric opened the door and led her inside. Summer went straight to one of the booths and sat down. Then she gave him her order. "I'll have two fish tacos, no picante. I hate picante."

Eric just looked at her. Then shook his head again.

"What now?" Summer asked in response to his head tick. "You really need to get a new move."

"Get up," he said, holding out his hand.

"I'm tired. All this biking and walking. I thought we were going to try the tacos," Summer said, ignoring his hand.

Eric shook his head again and this time he grabbed her hand and pulled her out of the booth. "First we're going to make them," he said as Summer stood up.

"But isn't that like someone's job?"

"You and the Riviera. Spoiled."

"I am not. I just don't think it's right to steal someone else's job. That's why they have unions and stuff."

"I know them," he said with a laugh. "And they like it when I visit and help."

Just then a boy about their age came out from the back. "Eric, you never can stay away, can you?" the boy said as he shook Eric's hand and patted him on the shoulder in the sort of man-hug old friends gave each other. "And you broughta lady."

Summer stood sheepishly behind Eric. "This is Summer," Eric said.

Summer stepped forward and shook the guy's hand. He introduced himself as Jay.

"Summer's from France," Eric said. "She's staying at the 'scape with me. Thought I'd show her around."

"I, um," Summer started to mumble in an attempt to correct the lie. She wasn't from France, Eric knew that. Why had he decided to play this game? She started to respond, but Eric cut her off as he grabbed her hand and they followed Jay into the back.

In the back there were several giant stoves, ovens, and deep fryers. It smelled of grease and cheese and chicken. Summer took in her surroundings. She had never been in the kitchen of a restaurant before. Normally she sat at a table and had a waiter serve her food. But now—

"Here's your apron. And the sink's over there. You have to wash before you cook," Jay said as he handed her a white canvas apron and pointed to the sink.

Summer looked to Eric for help but all he did was smile and shake his head. She smiled back. She was starting to catch on now. Whenever he shook his head like that it meant that he didn't approve of whatever she was doing at the moment. His comment from earlier replayed in her head. She wasn't spoiled like he had said. She had to prove him wrong. So she took the apron and tied it around her waist, then washed her hands.

"Where do I start?" she asked with a huge grin directed at Eric. Two could play this game.

"Over here," Jay shouted from the other side of the kitchen.

As Summer approached him, he threw a tennis-sized ball of dough at her. "Catch." Summer reached out her hands as the dough slapped into her palms. "Nice catch," Jay said.

"Thanks," Summer responded. "So now what?" she asked as she played with the dough, squishing it between her fingers.

"Not like that," Eric said as he approached from behind her. "People have to eat that."

"Hey, yell at the pitcher, not me," Summer said, smiling at Jay.

"She's funny," Jay said to Eric.

Eric nodded. Summer looked at him and waited for the head shake. But he didn't do it. Just smiled at her.

So Summer smiled back, then looked to Jay and held out her hands full of dough. "So seriously, what do I do with this?"

Jay took the dough from her hands and placed it on what appeared to be a large round pancake griddle. Then he pulled a metal lever and lowered another piece of metal down on top of the dough. Flattening it. And when he pulled the two round pieces apart all that was left was a perfectly baked tortilla.

"That's how you make those?" Summer asked. Jay nodded, then stepped away to give Summer a chance to make her own. She placed another ball of dough onto the hot metal and pulled the lever. When she was done, she revealed her own perfect tortilla. "Cool," she said. "So is this like your summer job?" she asked Jay.

Jay hesitated, then Eric stepped forward and answered for him.

"No. He works here all year. This is his parents' business. He helps them out."

"I get it," Summer started. "My friend Marissa, when her mom remarried, she married this guy, Caleb Nichol, and he has a family business. My other friend Seth, well, his mom is Caleb's daughter and she works there, too."

Eric just stared at her.

"Yeah, I know. Totally confusing. We're all like related somehow. You should've seen what happened when we found out Caleb's illegitimate daughter was our friend Lindsay."

"Caleb Nichol. As in the Newport Group?" Jay asked before Eric had a chance to respond.

"Um, yeah," Summer replied, realizing that she had totally blown her cover. Now Eric knew where she was really from, and that she had gone on a vacation ten minutes from home.

She looked at Eric, who was shaking his head. The disapproving tick. Dammit. She'd done it again.

"You're from Newport?" he asked. Summer nodded. "Isn't that just a few miles north of here?" Again she nodded. "Interesting."

Summer thought for a moment about her response. What would she say? But then . . . why did she say anything? It didn't really matter. He was the one who had assumed she was from somewhere exotic.

So she gave him no response and continued to help Jay make tortillas. Dough ball upon dough ball. The heat from the metal griddle making her face sweat. After Summer had made about thirty tortillas, she turned to Eric and asked if they could go.

Summer thanked Jay for letting them hang out and promised to stop by sometime with her friends.

Once they reached the bikes, Summer finally broke the silence.

"You know, I didn't lie. You're the one who assumed I was from someplace else."

"I know. I'm not mad."

"Good. Then why have you been so quiet?" Summer asked.

"Honestly? I'm starving. Being around all that food and not eating . . . kind of makes a guy hungry."

Summer felt her stomach rumble. "I'm so glad you said that. I'm starving. But I didn't want to be the first to say anything." Eric gave her an inquisitive look. "It's a girl thing," Summer said. He nodded. "Let's go back to the resort and we'll charge it to my room," she suggested.

The ride back to the resort felt much shorter. As they rode along the shore, Summer looked out at the empty waves and for the first time that afternoon, she remembered how Seth had ditched her. For a second she got angry again, but when she looked ahead and saw Eric goofing around on his bike the thought of Seth left her mind.

Back at Seascape, Summer and Eric left their bikes with the valet and headed inside to the little café overlooking the grounds.

Once they had ordered their food and the waiter had brought them bread, they both relaxed into their seats.

Summer stuffed a giant piece of bread into her mouth.

"You really were hungry," Eric said with a slight smile.

Summer smiled yeah. They laughed as crumbs fell onto her plate from the corners of her mouth.

"So, Newport," he began. Summer put another piece of bread into her mouth—anything to avoid having to talk.

"Yeah?" Summer finally said around a mouthful of bread. Then she waited for the head shake.

"What's it like?" he asked genuinely.

She was caught off guard. She had expected a full assault. A barrage of questions but not this one.

"You know. Typical town. Same old thing every day. A basic teenagers' life."

"I doubt that." Eric took a bite of bread.

"What do you mean?"

"Let's see. You live on a beach. Your school? Probably on a cliff somewhere overlooking the ocean. Kids surf and skate and play water polo. And I'm sure you don't even know what a snow day is."

Summer shook her head no. How would she know?

"It's when school gets canceled because there's too much snow on the ground and it's unsafe to drive in the weather," Eric explained.

"That happened to us, too."

"It snowed in Newport?"

"No. There was a recall of several Mercedes models brakes. It was unsafe to drive so they canceled school."

"You drive a Mercedes?"

"That was in fourth grade. All our parents did."

"Oh," Eric said. He laughed and shook his head.

"Okay, seriously. What is with that head shake? Am I doing something wrong?"

"No. You're funny. You're an original, Summer. You really are."

"Is that your nice way of saying I'm superficial?"

"And you're perceptive. Yeah."

"That's okay. I know I am. But there's more to me than that."

"Really?"

"Of course. You just haven't seen it yet."

"Well, then I guess you'll have to show me the other side of Summer. The less shallow side."

"Is that a challenge?" Summer asked.

Eric thought for a second as the waiter delivered their food. "I guess it is. Do you accept?"

And just as Summer was about to say yes, she saw Seth out of the corner of her eye.

"What the—?" She asked, spitting out her food as Seth approached their table. "Seth, what are you doing here?"

"I came to apologize for leaving you all alone. But obviously you've already taken care of that," Seth said as he glared at Eric.

"Eric, this is Seth. My friend. Excuse his manners. He's normally a bit nicer than this. Eric, do you mind? We'll be right back."

Eric gestured for them to go right ahead. Summer stood up and ushered Seth out of the restaurant.

"So, who's your new friend?" Seth asked jeasously.

"Someone I met after you ditched me."

"I didn't ditch you. The sail was all tangled and tattered and . . . I tried to call . . . but I lost my cell phone. . . ."

"Save it, Cohen. You totally ditched me. I made do. What other choice did I have? I wasn't about to become best friends with the stepmonster."

"But I . . . and the boat . . ."

"You and the damn boat. Last time you sailed away on it. This time you never even made it out of the harbor," Summer pointed out.

"Summer, please . . ."

"Look, I'm going back to my meal. I'll see you when I get home. In a few days."

Seth had nothing more to say. He couldn't say any more. And so he left.

Summer returned to the table and apologized to Eric. Then she suggested that maybe they should just call it a day.

So Eric left as well.

Leaving Summer all alone.

That evening Summer called Marissa.

"Why didn't you tell me that Seth was on his way?"

"I did," Marissa said. "I sent you a text message."

Summer went to her bag and pulled out her cell phone. "I totally forgot to turn my cell back on."

She turned on her phone and noticed that she had five messages and several texts. *Oops,* she thought. Seth had tried to call her.

"Why does it matter? I thought you were lonely there anyways," Marissa said.

"I was. I mean I am. But you know me—I hate surprises."

"That's not true. You love surprises." Marissa paused for a second, then continued. "You met someone, didn't you?"

Summer hesitated before answering. "Okay. I did. But he's just a friend. I got desperate. There was no one to hang out with."

"Is he cute?" Marissa asked.

"Yeah, I guess he is," Summer replied as she pictured Eric's face in her mind. He was. And nice. And funny and . . . Oh, no . . .

"I should go. I can hear the stepmonster calling. I'll call you tomorrow."

"Later," Marissa said.

As Summer hung up, she started to wonder, was she falling for Eric?

7

Meanwhile Seth was having a meltdown—and looking for sympathy. "He was hot, Ryan. Not that I was checking him out, but I know a good-looking man when I see one. And he wasn't the waspy version of me, like Zach. He was different. Like he wasn't from here," Seth said, pacing back and forth, wandering the kitchen.

"Was he foreign?"

"Not that I could tell." Seth paused. "Wait, what does that have to do with it?"

"I don't know. Just thought I'd ask." Ryan went to the cabinet and chose a box of cereal, his favorite nighttime snack.

"Focus, Ryan. Focus. What am I going to do? I tried to rescue her and the sail and the rudder and everything was such a disaster and I don't think she believed anything I said." Seth grabbed the box of cereal and pulled out a giant mixing bowl. All this worrying had made him hungry.

"You and Summer and boats really don't seem

to mix too well. Maybe you should start there." Ryan poured milk in his bowl.

"What else do I got, though? A skateboard? My iPod? Captain Oats?" Seth thought about his plastic toy horse. Then remembered that he had taken Princess Sparkles just in case. "Just in case this sort of thing happened," he said slowly.

"What are you talking about?"

"That's it." Seth spilled his cereal everywhere as he shot out of his seat.

"What's it?"

"Princess Sparkles. I took her just in case this sort of thing happened."

"What are you going to do? Hold her for ransom? Send a note that says if you don't come back here, you'll never see your horse again?"

"Of course not. That's ridiculous. I'm going to use the horse as an excuse to go back there," Seth said, the wheels spinning in his head.

"I don't know, Seth. She told you that she'd see you when she got back. Maybe you should just wait. Sleep on it. You've already been there once today. Remember last time when you chased her down? Zach almost hit you with his car."

"True. That would have been a mess. You're right. I'll start off slow. I'll call her tomorrow," Seth said, backing off the mission.

"Good. Now can we eat in peace?" Ryan took a bite of his cereal.

"And then if she doesn't respond, I'm going there."

"Seth, you two aren't even—"

"Ryan. Snack time. I don't want to hear it. We'll talk after the call tomorrow," Seth said as he thought about his plan to call Summer. And, of course, the backup plan of Princess Sparkles.

THE OC

8

A bummed-out Seth lay on his bed, searching. The ceiling above him was empty. No answers. No promises. Nothing. He hadn't moved an inch since Summer had hung up on him and that had been an hour ago.

"Seth, are you ready?" It was Ryan. Still Seth didn't move. Ryan let himself in and started, "Hey, you ready? I thought we were going to go to the Crab Shack for—" Then he stopped at the sight of Seth sprawled on the bed. "What happened to you?"

"Summer," was all Seth could mutter.

Ryan pulled out the chair from Seth's desk and sat down.

"Again? Really? I thought you were going to call her and apologize."

"What do you think I did, Ryan?" Seth asked, barely lifting his head to look at him. "She didn't want to hear it."

"Are you going to sit in here and mope all night?"

"Maybe," Seth whispered.

"That's pathetic. What happened to kicking off the summer of Seth and Ryan?"

"Summer happened. That's what, Ryan," Seth replied as he finally dragged himself into a seated position.

"Then so what," Ryan said, picking up Captain Oats from the bedside table and starting to play with it. Seth took notice.

"No. He can't play. He's depressed, too," Seth said as he took back his plastic horse.

"I thought he had Princess Sparkles?" Ryan asked with a smile. "A horse can't be down if he's got his match."

"Is this some sort of psychobabble you're trying to work on me?" Ryan nodded yes. Seth sat quiet for a second, then began, "Well, it's working. You're right. Call Marissa."

"What? Why?" Ryan asked, not expecting to have to drag her into Seth's mess, too.

"Because they're best friends. Marissa will know everything. We'll drill her, and then we'll go see Summer tomorrow and reunite her with Princess Sparkles and me."

"If I do this, there's no we. I'm not going there," Ryan said as he reached for the phone.

"Fine. I'll go see Summer by myself. But first, you have to call Marissa."

The boys shook on it. Seth would go see Summer alone the next day, and Ryan would call Marissa.

By the time Marissa arrived, Ryan couldn't hang out in Seth's room any longer. He had heard enough of Seth's music and needed something more than a few guitars and a raspy voice.

"We're going to the Crab Shack," Ryan said as he grabbed Marissa and pulled her away from the den of hell that Seth's room had become over the course of thirty minutes.

Marissa just nodded and followed Ryan out the door, with Seth walking close behind.

After they had ordered, Seth decided to get into the real purpose of inviting Marissa to hang out with them.

"So, Marissa," Seth began, "have you talked to Summer lately?"

"If you're asking me if she talked about you, then no. I'm staying out of it."

"Good call," Ryan said to Marissa as he reached for a roll and dipped it into the clam chowder the waiter had just delivered. Marissa grabbed a roll, too, and started eating her soup.

"Oh, so now you're both going to try and ignore me," Seth said as he, too, started spooning soup into his mouth. "Fine. Three can play that game."

And so the threesome sat in silence until the waiter delivered the rest of their food. Then Seth, who was a talker, couldn't take it any longer.

"Okay. You win. But can't you just help me out a little bit? I want things to go back to the way they were."

"Really?" Marissa asked as she took a bite of her fish. Ryan looked to Seth, curious as to what he would say.

"Well. No. I don't know. I just hate when Summer's mad at me. I'm not the same Seth. I'm quiet. Demure. It's not pretty, Marissa. You have to help me," Seth begged.

"I don't know, Ryan. What do you think?"

"A quiet Seth isn't always a bad thing," Ryan said with a wink and a laugh.

"Ryan, you remember what I did with Alex. I don't *do* bad boy. It turns into a mess. You can't have me quiet. I end up arrested."

"He does have a point," Ryan said to Marissa.

Marissa nodded. "Okay, I'll help you. But what do you want me to do?"

"Call her."

"And then what?" Marissa asked.

"Find out how her day was, act normal. Then see if she says anything about me."

Reluctantly Marissa said fine and dialed Summer's cell phone, secretly hoping that Summer had turned it off again.

But Summer picked up after two rings.

"Marissa," she exclaimed. "I was just about to call you. I have so much to tell you."

"Really?" Marissa asked as she looked over and saw Seth staring her down intently, hanging on every word she said.

"Remember that boy I told you about?"

"Yes." Seth gave Marissa a look that said, *you*

have to say more if I'm ever going to understand anything. Marissa held up her finger, telling Cohen to have patience. Ryan just continued to eat his dinner and shake his head. How did Seth get himself into these situations?

"He's seriously perfect. We had the most amazing day ever. If I ever make fun of the flyover zone again, shoot me. And he has the best body," Summer said on the other end of the call.

"Interesting," Marissa said, trying not to give away the fact that Summer was going on and on about Eric and not Seth. Seth continued to stare intently.

"Coop, what's wrong with you?" Summer asked, sensing Marissa's uneasiness.

"Nothing. Sorry. Well, that sounds good," Marissa said, hoping not to arouse Seth's suspicions. But Seth immediately went into a flurry of hand gestures trying to sign a message to Marissa but all it did was confuse her. She put up her finger again and tried to silence him.

"Just good?" Summer began, but was interrupted by a knock at the door. "Hold on, I think that's the monster. I'll be right back."

Marissa covered the phone and turned to Seth. "Stop that. I can't do this if you're over there flailing around. She's going to know. And I will so be dead. I can't believe I'm doing this."

"I'll buy your dinner," Seth said with puppy-dog eyes.

"Just keep quiet," Marissa hushed. Seth made the gesture as if he was zipping up his lips and throwing away the key.

"All right, I'm back," Summer said and Marissa uncovered the phone. "That was weird. It was the bellboy with a message. I think it was from Eric. We made plans for tomorrow. I think it was a hint."

"What'd it say?" Marissa asked. This threw Seth even further into a spiral of curiosity, but Marissa gave him the evil eye and he made the key gesture again.

"It didn't say anything," Summer replied. "It was just a hammer and a box of red nails."

"That's weird," Marissa replied. "Maybe it has some significance."

"Well, obviously. I guess I'll have to wait. That's my new thing, Coop. I'm just waiting for life to guide me. Direct me as to where to go."

Marissa thought about her friend's new philosophy for a moment. "I like it," she said. "I think I might try that. Think it will work on evil mothers?"

"Haven't tried it on the monster yet."

"Let me know how it goes."

"I will. Speaking of the monster, I hear her calling. It's feeding time. Something with the meds."

"Call me tomorrow and let me know how it goes," Marissa said.

"Of course. 'Night, Coop."

"'Night," Marissa said as she hung up the phone and placed it back in her purse. Then she went back to eating as though she had never had the conversation.

"Oh, no, you can't do that," Seth said as he unlocked his lips.

"I said I'd call her, find out how her day was. Never said I'd say anything." Marissa took another bite.

"That's not fair," Seth whined as he pushed away his half-eaten plate of salmon. Marissa continued to eat her fish and looked to Ryan to help her.

"How about a compromise?" Ryan suggested. "Seth, you can ask Marissa one question and she'll answer it. But that's it. One question."

"Fine," Marissa began, "but just one. I'm not losing her as a friend just because you're neurotic."

Seth agreed and thought long and hard for several minutes before asking his question. "All right. I got it. What was so weird?"

"Oh, that," Marissa started, thinking Seth had completely asked the wrong question. This wouldn't give anything away. "The bellboy delivered a hammer and a box of red nails to her room."

"What does that mean?" Seth asked.

"Exactly why I said it was weird," Marissa said, returning to her dinner.

"That's not weird," Ryan suddenly said.

"What?" Seth asked as he turned to him. Marissa almost choked on her fish. Did Ryan know about Eric? Was it some secret brotherhood guys had when they weren't from Newport?

"Yeah, everyone who volunteers for Houses for

Friends gets that delivered the night before they go in to work."

"Summer's a volunteer?" Seth asked, slightly surprised. "I guess she was pretty handy that time she and I fixed up your room," Seth said as he looked at Marissa.

Marissa nodded and tried to hide her expression behind her fork. She didn't want to give her friend away. But Seth was too observant.

"Uh-uh," he started. "You're hiding something. What do you know?"

Marissa looked to Ryan for help.

"You had your one question. That's it. Can we order dessert?" Ryan asked, trying to help her. Marissa signaled for the waiter.

But Seth wasn't giving up that easily. "I don't trust it. I'm going there."

"No you're not. You don't know how to use a hammer," Ryan said. "And you can't stalk her. That's weird."

"You're right," Seth conceded. "But you can. You worked construction. It won't seem weird if you go."

"This sounds like a bad idea," Ryan said and this time he looked to Marissa for help.

"I agree," she began. "But I'm staying out of this. This is all you two."

Seth gave Ryan a pleading look. "Princess Sparkles, Captain Oats. We all need our mates, Ryan. We can't lose them to a construction site. What if there's an accident?"

"Seth."

"Please. I'll do your chores for a month."

"We don't have chores. We have a maid." Ryan laughed.

"Right. Well, if we did, I'd do them," Seth pleaded. And kept on pleading for twenty minutes.

"Fine. But you owe me big," Ryan said, finally giving in.

"I had nothing to do with this," Marissa added. Both boys looked to her. "In case anyone asks. I'm staying out of your messes."

Both boys agreed and the three left to prepare for the next day.

Marissa sent Summer a text message saying sorry for Cohen. She hoped that Summer would check it.

9

Summer showed up at Eric's dressed in one of her-best designer outfits. Her hair was straight, her makeup perfect. She was ready for their date. She still hadn't figured out what the hammer and the nails meant but figured Eric had some clever explanation. Something poetic or romantic. Something very un-Cohen.

Maybe red nails were some ancient sign for luck or love or lucky in love. Either way, she was ready to find out. She tousled her hair and applied one last coat of lip gloss, then she knocked on the door. A butterfly fluttered in her stomach, but she took a deep breath and silenced it.

Then Eric opened the door. She smiled but he didn't smile back. Just took one look at her and shook his head. "You can't wear that," he said.

Summer looked down at her miniskirt and tank top and was offended. Since when did some guy from Chicago have better style than she did?

"Well, I think it's cute," Summer said.

"Never said it wasn't," Eric began. "But didn't you get the package?"

"The hammer and nails? Yeah. But what does that have to do with my outfit?" Summer asked as she waited for Eric to give her his poetic response. The hidden meaning of it all. The romantic gesture.

"It's Houses for Friends," Eric explained as he motioned for Summer to enter.

Summer followed him inside, then asked, "What's that?"

"It's a charity."

"Oh," Summer began as Eric led her up the stairs. "I love that kind of stuff. We do charity events all the time in Newport. So what's this about?"

"It's a house-building program," Eric said as he brought Summer into his room and started going through his closet.

"Cool," Summer said, watching Eric throw old T-shirts and shorts onto the bed. "So, do they, like, have people bid on new homes and a portion of the sales goes to charity?"

"Not exactly," Eric started as he held clothes up to Summer's body until he finally found a pair of shorts and a T-shirt that was close to her size. "Here. These should work."

"For what?" Summer asked as she looked down at the oversized T-shirt and shorts. "The maid?"

"For building a house," Eric replied matter-of-factly. "Hurry up and change. We're going to be late."

And before Summer had a chance to respond, Eric was out the door, leaving her to change.

She looked in the mirror at the great outfit she was already wearing. *What a waste*, she thought. All that time spent this morning picking out the perfect skirt and top and now she was going to have to change into these ratty old clothes. How was Eric supposed to find her attractive if she was wearing them?

Then she noticed a pair of scissors on the dresser and had an idea. If she had to wear these clothes, she'd make them her own.

She quickly got to work, cutting the T-shirt into a sexy little tank top, which she tied at the top so that one side hung off her shoulder just a bit. Then she moved on to the shorts, which were way too long. She cut the hem so that her legs were visible, then she found some safety pins in one of the dresser drawers and tightened the waist so that the-shorts hugged her hips.

Not too bad, she thought as she looked at her new outfit in the mirror. It was almost trendy and cute.

"You ready?" Eric called from outside the door.

"Just about," Summer called back as she took one last look in the mirror. Not perfect, but at least it was better than what he had handed her.

Summer opened the door and smiled at Eric.

"Wow," Eric said as he checked her out. "Hope you're this handy with a hammer and nails."

"So are we just, like, decorating the house for poor people?" Summer asked as she followed him down the stairs. "'Cause I can build shelves and hang pictures. I'm actually pretty—"

"No. We're building the house."

"The entire thing?" Summer asked, growing concerned that she had gotten herself in way over her head.

"Pretty much," Eric replied with a smile.

Summer smiled back. Whatever her concerns, it was too late to back out now. And besides, Eric had issued her a challenge to prove that she wasn't always shallow and superficial and this would be a good way to prove him wrong.

As long as there wasn't any heavy lifting.

10

"So I've pretty much done all the heavy lifting," Seth said as he pushed his chair back from his desk and turned to face Ryan, who was sitting on the bed in his usual white tank top and a pair of worn jeans. "The site is just outside Riverside."

"I still can't believe you convinced me to do this," Ryan sighed.

"Ryan, we're brothers. This is what brothers do."

"Really?" Ryan began. "I thought we were supposed to fight. Play sports. Talk about girls."

"No. We're Cohens. It's more complicated than that." Seth turned back to the desk and hit PRINT on the computer.

"Right. We stalk girls for each other."

"It's not stalking, Ryan. It's you doing something nice. Donating your time for charity. It just so happens that I have good reason to believe that Summer's going to be there. *And* if my suspicion happens to be true, then I give you permission to ask about me."

"It's not a suspicion when you force Marissa to

tell you Summer's whereabouts," Ryan said as he stood up and got the directions from the printer.

"You and the details. Regardless, you're still going. So, here's the plan. I'll drive you out there, drop you off several blocks away, and then once you spot Summer and you get in her good graces, you can bring her to the car, where I'll be waiting with Princess Sparkles. Then we'll make up and, if all goes as planned, we'll all return to Newport together."

"Doesn't she have to go back to Seascape with her family?"

"Again with the details. We really need to break you of that habit," Seth said, snatching the directions out of Ryan's hands.

Ryan just shook his head and prepared for the worst. Seth's plans usually *turned out* badly but this one had already started out bad.

11

After what was in Summer's opinion, the bus ride from hell, she and Eric arrived at a construction site somewhere in the Inland Empire. A place Summer had never been before, a place a world away from Newport.

"We could have borrowed my dad's car, you know," Summer said as they exited the bus. She covered her nose as the bus belched exhaust fumes into the air.

Eric looked at the crowd of people gathered around at the site. "Not the best way to make friends around here. Besides, what if there's another recall on Mercedes? Wouldn't want to get in an accident."

"So now you're the funny one?" Summer exclaimed as she took a good look at her surroundings. This wasn't exactly an episode of *Trading Spaces*. There was no hot carpenter and no host wearing a cute shirt and designer jeans. Most of the girls here had their hair pulled back in ponytails and were dressed in old T-shirts and shorts much like the ones Eric had tried to get her to wear earlier. Summer looked down at the clothes she had fashioned out of his and for the first time in her life she felt out of place. "Are you sure about this?" Summer asked. It was definitely too late to back out now, but she had to try.

"Come on. It'll be fun. Trust me."

"There's been a lot of trusting around here lately," Summer said. She looked to Eric for some reassurance. Something to make her keep moving forward and enable her to join the crowd.

"And you're still alive," he said as he reached down and grabbed her hand. "Let's go."

Summer felt his cool palm against hers and took a deep breath. That was all the reassurance she needed.

They joined the crowd just as the site leader stood up to give them their instructions for the day.

Summer looked at everyone around her and wondered where all these people came from. They were definitely not from Newport, she could tell that much for sure. But how did so many people know about this Houses for Friends thing? Summer was actually kind of impressed by the fact that Eric seemed to know a lot about this area even though he only lived there part-time. She'd lived nearby all her life and had no idea that this stuff happened. It was like an alternate universe.

"Thank you all so much for coming. It's so great to have you all out to help. For some of you this is your first time. And for others this has become your regular summer gig," the leader said as he smiled at Eric. Summer looked over at him and he smiled at her. Apparently he was a regular here. Another thing about him that she hadn't known. "For those of you who are new . . ." Eric squeezed Summer's hand. She squeezed back. ". . . we work in teams. Some of you will be moving lumber. Others will be in charge of construction and, if all goes as planned, by the end of the day we will need to form a decorating team that can start painting and installing carpet. . . ." *That*, Summer thought, *is something I can do*. She was good at decorating. And she enjoyed it and as far as she knew there was no lifting involved. "So I'm going to ask for the veterans here to pair up with someone new and help direct us into teams." Summer held on tight to Eric's hand so as not to lose him as the leader finished and said, "But most of all, enjoy and have fun!" Everyone cheered and then began to break off into groups.

Summer tried to find the decorating group but Eric tightened his grip on her hand and led her over to a group that was gathering around stacks of lumber. Construction. Physical labor.

"I don't know if I can . . ." Summer started, not really wanting to get sweaty. It was hot out here away from the ocean. But Eric just dropped her hand and placed a finger on her lips to silence her.

"This is the best part," he started. "And the most rewarding."

"But I think I'd be better at decorating,"

Summer pleaded, remembering all the feng shui guides she had read over the past year.

"If you don't have walls, what are you going to decorate?" Eric laughed.

"You have a point. But . . ."

"Are you wimping out on me?" Eric asked with a smile. Summer took a moment to think, once again remembering his challenge. Maybe she would just have to suck it up and do the work. It wasn't like she didn't know how to use a hammer, it was just that she was afraid that this kind of work was going to be extremely labor-intensive. She wasn't cut out for construction. She'd certainly checked out construction workers when they were tan and sweaty and shirtless, she'd even imagined what it'd be like to make out with one of them, but she never imagined that she'd actually *be* a construction worker.

Eric stood there staring at her, waiting for an answer.

"No, I'm not wimping out on you," she replied. She had to face the challenge and prove Eric wrong. And maybe then when he discovered that there was more to her than her apparently superficial surface he would kiss her. That was all she really wanted. One little kiss. Something to make her forget that Cohen had ditched her. Something to make this vacation worthwhile.

"Good," Eric said as he handed her a hammer and a tool belt with a pouch full of nails connected to it.

"I think fanny packs already came and went," Summer started as she examined the tool belt. "Twice," she finished as she handed the belt back to Eric. It didn't really go with her outfit.

"You're going to need that," Eric said as he turned her around and fastened the belt around her waist.

"Fine," she said, "but I'm not lifting anything."

"Of course not. You'd collapse," Eric said as he squeezed her tiny waist. "You need some more meat on your bones before we let you do that. Right, guys?" Eric asked loudly to the group.

Summer tried to smile as everyone stared at her. She wasn't sure whether or not to take Eric's comment as an insult or a compliment. But she decided to just take it in stride and go with it.

"So what's my job?" Summer asked enthusiastically, hammer in hand, tool belt on waist.

All the guys at the construction site stared at the sight of her in her little shorts and tank top, holding up her hammer. Summer felt them gazing at her and wondered if the shirtless workers she normally gazed at felt the same way she did now.

"You're the cutest little construction worker I've ever seen," Eric said before placing a hard hat on her head.

"Thanks." Summer smiled. With Eric nearby, she felt less out of place than she had before, and now that she knew how to get the men's attention she figured she could get out of any heavy lifting or anything else that would make her sweat.

All the volunteers got to work and slowly but surely the construction site began to resemble a home. Summer was actually pretty proud of herself for being a part of the experience. She'd hung shelves and photos before but actually building a house was amazing and she felt good about it.

She'd never been involved in a charity that produced tangible results. Usually it was a fashion show or bake sale or kissing booth to raise money, nothing as grand as building a house for a family in need.

As she continued to hammer nail after nail, she even started to forget that she was on a miserable vacation with her dad and stepmother, and that Cohen had ditched her. She liked Eric. He forced her to forget all the things that had worried her at the beginning of this trip. And now as she glanced at him, working, his shirt off and his muscles glistening in the hot sun, she wondered if she was worthy of his kiss yet. If he had found her to be more than just a superficial beauty.

And just as her mind began to imagine what a kiss from Eric might be like, she snapped back into reality.

It was Ryan. Working on the other side of Eric. What was he doing here? She knew that he had worked construction last summer, but what a coincidence that he just happened to show up to volunteer on the same day that she randomly got dragged into this, too. And that he'd joined the same crew that she'd joined. And that he was working right near her . . .

Summer continued to hammer away, head down, attempting to hide. Maybe if Ryan didn't see her, she wouldn't have to explain what she was doing here. Maybe she wouldn't have to explain *who* she was here with. It wasn't like there was anything wrong with what she was doing—she was doing something really good, noble even. And it wasn't like there was something going on between her and Eric . . . at least, not yet . . . but somehow she didn't know if Ryan would see it that way. More important, she *knew* that Seth wouldn't see it that way, when Ryan mentioned running into her at the site, which he was bound to do. After all, what were the chances that Summer Roberts would be working construction, even if it was for a good cause? Ryan was sure to say something and then Cohen would go off on one of his weird mind trips. It was too horrible to think about. Then another horrible thought crossed her mind: What would everyone back at Harbor think if they knew that she had been engaged in manual labor? It would *so* not help her image! She kept hammering but her concentration was off. Something had to give, and give it did.

"Ouch," Summer screamed as she accidentally hammered her thumb into the wood. Everyone, including Ryan, looked at her, doubled over in pain, her hand throbbing. Eric immediately came to her aid and gave her finger a once-over.

"I think you're okay. Doesn't look broken. Just going to be a nasty bruise," he said.

"Yeah. You want some ice?" another voice asked. Summer looked up to say that she would be fine, she didn't need ice, just a short break. But when she looked up she saw that it was Ryan.

"Ryan! What are you doing here?" she asked, trying to seem surprised, trying to cover the fact that she had been hiding from him.

"I, uh," he stuttered. "You know. Just thought I'd do a little work for charity. I started to miss the old job, so Kirsten sent me out here."

Summer could tell that he was lying, but she wasn't sure if she could call him on it. She didn't really want to get in to it and embarrass herself in front of Eric. Not any more than she already had.

"That was nice of her. I, uh . . ." Summer paused. Should she introduce Ryan to Eric? At this point she kind of had to. After all, they were standing next to each other. "Ryan, this is Eric. We met at Seascape. His stepmonster dragged him there, too."

"It's not as bad as she makes it seem," Eric said to Ryan as they shook hands.

"That's what I figured," Ryan said, eyeing Summer, then looking back at Eric. "So you two are—?"

"Friends," Summer said quickly. Maybe too quickly because Ryan got a suspicious look on his-face.

"Yeah," Eric added. "Had to show Summer a little more of the world, you know?"

Ryan laughed.

"Hey," Summer exclaimed. "I'm hurt here. It's not nice to make fun of the disabled."

Eric bent down and kissed her thumb. "There. All better."

Summer looked at him with a smile, the feel of his lips still lingering on her hand. Then she shook her head as she remembered that Ryan was standing there. Did he notice?

"So, are you guys going to be here tomorrow?" Ryan asked, looking directly at Summer. "Because I was thinking about bringing Seth. It'd be good for him. Maybe we could all—"

Oh, no, Summer thought. Did Seth send Ryan here to spy on her? But how had he even know where she was? This was too weird.

"No," Summer replied quickly. "I think I have to spend time with the monster tomorrow. Speaking of the monster—" Summer turned to Eric. "I never told her where I was going today. We should really get back."

"Um, okay." Eric hesitated. Summer stood up and grabbed his hand.

"It was good to see you, though, Ryan. Tell everyone I said hi," she said as she walked off with Eric in tow.

He kept trying to talk, but all Summer could do was put her finger to his lips to keep him silent.

Once they were out of sight, she told him that she would explain once they got back to the resort.

"And how are we going to get there?" he asked.

"Cab, of course," Summer said.

"There are no cabs out here," Eric replied.

"Then I guess we'll just have to . . ." Summer looked around for a solution, but all she could see was the bus stop. "Take the bus."

"I thought you didn't . . ."

"I'm roughing it. Less superficial. More Summer," she said as she darted across the street to the bus stop and took a seat on the bench.

"Whatever you say," Eric said as he sat down beside her.

Summer looked back down the street but the new house was out of view. Hopefully, Ryan couldn't see them. Then she looked around. If Ryan was here, Seth couldn't be too far away. And for a moment she felt like she was being spied on. That Seth was hiding behind a bush somewhere watching. Waiting. Ready to pounce.

12

"You have officially lost it. What are you doing?" Ryan asked as he approached Seth's car only to find him hiding behind a bush holding a pair of binoculars.

"Shhhh. Don't blow our cover," Seth whispered.

"Seth. Get out of there. Let's go," Ryan said, still standing.

"You failed the mission, Ryan. I'm just trying to clean up your mess." Seth put the binoculars back up to his face and eyed Summer and Eric.

"What are you going to do? Sit there and spy on her all day?" Ryan reached for the binoculars, but Seth pulled them away.

"No. Of course not. She's getting on a bus. She won't be here all day."

"Great. Well, that doesn't sound stalkerish at all. Give me the keys," Ryan said, holding out his hand.

"Where are you going?"

"Home. I can't do this anymore." Ryan turned to walk away.

"You didn't do anything. Except help to build a house for a needy family," Seth told him.

"Seth, I'm pretty sure she caught on. She's smarter than you think."

"Shit!" Seth screamed. "Duck." Then he reached up and pulled Ryan down into the bushes with him.

"What are we—"

Seth shushed Ryan again. Then the giant bus came rolling by. When it had passed, Seth asked, "Do you think she saw us?"

Ryan looked up at the giant Range Rover behind them. "No. Definitely didn't see us. Our car? Yes."

"I'm screwed, aren't I?" Seth asked, sinking to the ground.

"Depends on how strict the stalker laws are in California," Ryan said as he stood up.

"Great. Thanks. I'll see you in ten years," Seth said, defeated.

"Come on. Let's get out of here," Ryan said as he grabbed the keys out of Seth's hand and got in the car. "Maybe she won't know."

"I highly doubt it," Seth sighed as he dragged himself into the car.

13

After a silent bus ride, Summer and Eric finally arrived back at the stop outside of Seascape.

"I can't believe him," Summer said.

"Who?" Eric asked as he helped her off the bus. "Your friend Ryan?"

"No. Yes." Summer shook her head, confused. "He's Seth's friend. They were spying on me. At least Seth was and somehow he got Ryan to help. I cannot believe him!"

Eric paused and gave her a strange look as they started the long walk up the drive to the resort.

"I showed you Seth's car on the way out," Summer explained, suddenly feeling like she had to prove that she wasn't imagining things.

"So is Seth your boyfriend?"

Summer hesitated, then began, "Technically, no. But we have this past. We were together once. Then twice."

"So why is he stalking you?"

"That's the thing about Seth. When we're together, he's great for a few weeks. Then he always finds a way to mess things up. And when we're not together, he becomes obsessed with me. Messes things up with new guys," Summer added.

"We usually want what we can't have," Eric told her as he reached down for her hand.

The butterflies reappeared in Summer's stomach. Was this it? Was this the moment where he declared her unsuperficial and kissed her? She took a deep breath and waited. But nothing happened.

Instead he held her hand up and started inspecting it. "It's not too bad," he said.

"What?" Summer asked, confused. Where was her kiss? Then she remembered the giant bruise that was probably forming on her thumb. She looked at it. He was right. It wasn't that bad. "Thanks," she said. Then she felt lame for causing so much drama earlier with Ryan and Seth and the bus . . . and everything. "I'm sorry about earlier," she said. "I did have fun today, though. Minus the stalkers." She had to redeem herself. She still wanted that kiss.

"Me, too." He smiled. Then he squeezed her hand and told her to put ice on her thumb. "I'll see you tomorrow?"

"Sure," Summer replied. "I'll be at the pool."

"See you then," he said as he ran off through the resort.

Summer watched him go and thought how great that first kiss would be. How sometimes the best things really did come to those who waited.

* * *

That night, Summer called Marissa to fill her in on the details of her day.

"You're never going to believe who stalked me today," Summer exclaimed.

"Seth," Marissa said flatly.

"How did you know?" Summer asked, a little bit of her enthusiasm diminished.

"He keeps bugging me, trying to find you," Marissa explained.

"You told him where I was?" Summer asked, starting to get a little bit upset. Why had her friend turned her in?

"No. They were with me last night when I talked to you and they overheard the part about the nails and the hammer. Don't be mad."

"So they figured the rest out on their own?"

"Yeah. Ryan knew about Houses for Friends."

"Figures," Summer said.

"So, tell me. How was it?" Marissa asked.

"Having Cohen stalk me?"

"No. Eric. How is he? Still cute?"

"Totally," Summer said as she felt her cheeks get red. "I'm meeting him again tomorrow."

"That sounds great," Marissa replied unenthusiastically, missing her friend.

"Hey, Coop. What have you been up to?"

"The usual. Avoiding my mom. Hiding in my room."

"I wish you were here," Summer said, feeling bad that her friend was so lonely without her. She had essentially ditched Marissa and made this whole trip all about herself and her own misery. Was Cohen rubbing off on her? Was she becoming selfish like him? "I'm sorry. I'll be back soon. Maybe you should come visit."

"We'll see. I think I have to help my mom with some fashion show thing or something. But we'll talk. No worries."

"You sure, Coop? I don't want to come home and find you hitting the bottle again."

"I won't be." Marissa laughed. "Besides, I'm sure the boys—well, Seth anyway—will be back soon to bug me again. I've got plenty to do. Good night."

"'Night," Summer said as she hung up the phone. She felt guilty that Marissa was stuck in Newport all alone while she was actually beginning to have a good time in Laguna, apart from the whole Seth stalker thing.

At least she would see Eric in the morning. . . .

14

The next morning Summer woke up to discover the stepmonster crawling all around her room. Literally crawling, down on the floor on her hands and knees. Even for the monster this was odd behavior.

"Hello?" Summer whispered, not wanting to shake her out of some sort of drug-induced nervous state. She'd done that once before by accident and the result hadn't been pretty. The monster had had to go on several different meds for a while, and Summer didn't want to be responsible for another trip to the hospital.

The monster turned around and leaned back on her calves. "I lost it."

Of course you have, Summer wanted to yell. *You're crawling on my floor.* But she held it in. "What?" she asked.

"My marriage."

"I don't think you lost it on my floor," Summer tried to explain nicely. Maybe she really had lost it.

"The ring," her stepmother said as she resumed crawling around, searching.

"Your wedding ring?" Summer asked, slowly catching on. "But how did it get in—"

"Please help me," the monster pleaded innocently, normally. And for the first time ever, Summer actually felt sorry for her stepmother. She could almost see tears forming in her eyes and she knew that it really was dire. The monster never cried. *Ever.* It was physically impossible with all the antidepressants she was on.

Summer climbed out of her warm bed and joined her stepmother on the floor to help search.

As they crawled around, Summer began to see that maybe underneath all the ailments, psychoses, and medications there was a real woman. She'd always seen her as, well, a monster. Someone who'd taken the place of her real mother. Someone who sort of just came along and filled a void in her father's life. But now as she saw how distraught her stepmother was about losing her wedding ring, she realized that maybe there was more to their marriage, and she started to really search for the ring.

She could see her stepmother slowly sinking into depression and Summer knew that she had to find the ring.

Slowly but surely the monster retreated into a corner of the room and began to cry. But her crying was devoid of any emotion. Her face was blank but the tears were flowing nonstop. Summer was scared. She had to find the ring.

She continued to search desperately. Under the bed. In the trash. Under the sheets. In the corners.

In the sink of the bathroom. She couldn't imagine why the ring would be in her room but it didn't matter; she had to keep searching.

Until. . . .

She spotted her stepmother's purse on a chair where she'd thrown it when she came in. Summer looked inside it. And of course there it was. Right on top of the wallet and makeup case. "I found it," she said as she cautiously approached the sobbing monster.

The tears seemed to stop instantaneously as Summer handed the ring over to her stepmother.

"Thank you," she whispered, then haphazardly pulled herself up from the ground and silently left the room.

"You're welcome," Summer whispered back as the door closed and she was all alone. Baffled. Wondering when things would be normal with her family. When they could go on real vacations.

Then Summer realized that she was supposed to meet Eric at the pool. Maybe it was shallow of her but suddenly that mattered more than anything, so putting aside thoughts of her stepmother, she quickly got ready and headed out the door.

As she was walking toward the pool, she ran into her dad and her stepmother, who had the biggest smile ever. Inside Summer felt satisfied that she had done something good.

And as they passed by each other, Summer told them both that she would be at the pool with Eric all day. They told her that they'd be playing tennis for a while and then they would be at the spa. She'd call or leave a note if she went anywhere. Then they parted and Summer saw her stepmother reach down and grab her dad's hand and for the first time in a long time, Summer found their love for each other endearing.

"Where've you been?" Eric asked as Summer approached his chair.

She thought about telling her crazy stepmother story, but she decided against it. It was their little secret. "Couldn't find my bikini bottom. I'm good now," she finally said.

"Good, because I've had enough of this pool," Eric said as he stood up and started to put his shirt on. *Wait*, Summer thought as she tried to catch one last glimpse of his defined abs.

"But I just got here," Summer pleaded, then sat down on the chair.

"I'm bored. How can you spend hours just lying in the sun?"

Summer hesitated. She'd never really thought about it before. Lying in the sun was just a summer ritual for her and Marissa. Just something they did. There really was no explanation. "I don't know."

"Besides, I have something else I want to show you," Eric said with a smile and held out his hand to help her up off the chair.

Summer looked up at him. *That hand,* she thought. Always coaxing her to do things. And again she couldn't resist. She reached up.

"As long as it doesn't involve tools and we don't have to bike there," she said, standing up.

"We won't. We'll—"

"Or take the bus," Summer added before he even finished his sentence.

Eric let go of her hand. "That's a long walk to town."

But Summer had had enough exercise this vacation. She had a better idea. "We can take my dad's car."

"The Mercedes? What if we crash?"

"We won't crash," Summer laughed. "Come on, they're playing tennis." This time it was she who reached out for Eric's hand and led him through the resort. She liked being in control.

When they found her dad and stepmother, Summer told her father that she and Eric were going into town.

At first, he was reluctant to let her take the car, but after some convincing from her stepmother, Summer was happily on her way to the valet with Eric in tow.

This time she had some control and if any more drama occurred or it turned out to be labor-intensive, she wouldn't have to take a bus to escape.

15

Ryan stood in the Cohen's garage trying to get his bike out from under the mess that had accumulated on top of it—white twinkle lights, extra chairs, all remnants from the parties Kirsten had hosted at the house over the past year.

Finally, Ryan managed to free his bike from the clutter and set off down the driveway just as Seth came running out the front door. He ignored Ryan and quickly jumped into the car. Ryan knew immediately that Seth was up to no good. This had to be some sort of extension of yesterday's disastrous encounter with Summer.

Ryan stepped in front of the car and motioned for Seth to stop.

"Where are you going?" he asked as Seth rolled down the window.

"Nowhere," Seth said quickly, trying to cover.

"You're going to see her. Aren't you?" Ryan asked in a stern voice.

"I have to," Seth relented. "She's going to think I'm a crazy stalker."

"And I'm sure she'll think you're normal if you show up there again."

"That's why I have to explain myself."

"So, you're going to stalk her to tell her that you're not a stalker?"

"No. Ryan. I'm going to her hotel. That's not stalking. She told me she was there. If you already know where they are, and they told you that they'd be there, then technically it's not stalking."

"I thought showing up unwanted and uninvited was the definition of stalking."

Seth glared at him. "Or maybe I'm wrong. Good luck, buddy," Ryan relented. There was no stopping Seth when he had a plan.

Seth started the car and began to back out of the driveway.

"Don't call me if you get arrested!" Ryan yelled after him, but Seth was too far away to hear. Just smiled, waved, and drove off into the sun.

Ryan shook his head, knowing that this was not going to end well.

16

"How cute," Summer exclaimed as she parked the car. Eric had directed Summer to a quaint little row of art galleries. They were situated off the main road and appeared to be old beach bungalows that had been moved to this location.

She ran up to the first window and peered in at several black-and-white photographs of exotic locations mixed in with colorful sunsets from around the world.

"Why couldn't I have gone there for vacation?" Summer wondered aloud as she pointed to a photo that looked like the Caymans.

"But then you and I never would have met," Eric said from behind her.

Summer took a step back. "Sorry," she started. "I didn't mean to say that aloud. No offense."

"None taken. How can I compete with that?" He pointed to a photo of the most gorgeous sunset Summer had ever seen. It looked like it was in Fiji or Thailand—somewhere exotic. The horizon was speckled with old fishing boats and the sky was shades of purple highlighted with pink and orange.

"You can't," Summer said with a sly smile. "Let's go in and look." She moved toward the front door, but Eric grabbed her hand and pulled her in the opposite direction.

"Later," he replied. *What next?* Summer wondered as she trailed behind him. Was she going to have to build something? Cook something? Maybe she had to milk a goat or chop down a tree . . . with Eric anything seemed possible. Summer reluctantly followed. Why couldn't they just enjoy what they had? Go to restaurants and shops and galleries like normal people.

Eric led her around the bungalow and into a small little cottage in the back of the gallery.

"What is this?" Summer asked. She looked all around and saw that this wasn't an extension of the gallery but rather what appeared to be an artist's studio. There were paints and canvases and easels full of unfinished work.

"Exactly what it seems," Eric replied as he entered and began to move several chairs and easels around.

"I don't think we should be here," she said. This was someone's office. Maybe even their home. She felt like she was intruding. All this art was personal. Like she had stepped inside someone else's life.

"It's okay. I come here all the time." Eric placed two chairs in front of a pair of empty easels.

"Is there anywhere you don't go all the time?" Summer asked, realizing that was essentially Eric's answer to everything. His explanation for everything they had done so far together over the past few days.

Eric thought for a few seconds, then replied, "Nope."

Then he went back to moving things around. Digging through cabinets and drawers until he produced a selection of paints and brushes.

Summer stood by watching him as he worked. Was he a painter too? What didn't this guy do?

"All set," he said and motioned for Summer to come over and sit in one of the chairs.

Summer didn't move. Ever since the second grade when J.D. Lewis ate a whole tube of red paint and vomited it up, she'd avoided art classes.

"I thought you were going to paint something. 'Mister I do this all the time,'" Summer said, trying to avoid having to sit. Easels, paints, canvas . . . it all made her feel kind of ill.

"We're both going to. Come on. Just sit." He went over and grabbed her by the forearm and led her to the chair. Summer sat on the very edge of it. Maybe, she thought, if she didn't sit fully on it, the nausea would die down.

Then Eric placed a brush in her hand and told her to start painting. "Broaden your horizons," he said.

But Summer didn't paint a thing. "What is this?" she asked. "Educate Summer week? First making the tortillas. Then the house building. Now the art. Are you trying to make me well-rounded?"

Eric laughed, then nodded. "Maybe."

"Well, I think I should stay the way I am—at least about art."

Eric shook his head. And dipped her paintbrush in some paint, then guided her hand and the brush over the canvas. "There. It's easy." He let go of her hand.

"That's all the help I get? Where's my muse? Nude model?"

Again Eric shook his head. But this time he didn't help her, just sat down in his chair and began to paint for himself.

"Great. Couldn't you at least have given me a paint-by-numbers canvas? *That* I can do."

"Just paint from the heart. Paint what you feel."

"If I painted what I felt, it'd be a big blob of nothing. Can I leave it blank?"

Eric shook his head no.

"What if I screw it up?" she asked, still unsure of this, still picturing J.D. vomiting red paint.

"You can't. There's no right or wrong. You wear makeup, right?"

Summer nodded.

"It's the same thing."

But Summer wasn't so sure. And she didn't want to embarrass herself in front of Eric. What if her painting was horrible? What if she couldn't pull this off in the least bit? This was part of the reason why she liked to come off as shallow and superficial. At least then no one expected her to be smart or artistic.

She looked over at Eric, who was shaking his head, and she felt even more self-conscious. If she didn't paint, he'd think she was unwilling to try new things·and if she did paint, she risked looking like a fool. Either way she was screwed.

So she decided to just go for it. Maybe she could do the whole Jackson Pollock thing and splatter paint everywhere. Or just paint the canvas all one color. That was probably a cop-out, but she had seen it done in certain home decorating magazines.

She picked up a new brush and dipped it in yellow. Then just started painting lines this way and that. Maybe she could re-create the sunset she had seen in the photograph in the front of the gallery.

And as she continued to paint she started to really get into it. And the more she painted, the more her canvas actually began to look like something distinguishable. She looked over at Eric, who had stopped shaking his head and had really gotten into his own painting.

She stared for a beat too long, because he eventually caught her looking at him, but he didn't freak out—just looked back at her and smiled. A heartfelt smile. She had made the right decision. Even if her canvas was awful at least he had stopped shaking his head.

Summer was actually enjoying this afternoon. Maybe educate Summer week wasn't so bad after all. Or so she thought . . .

But as she looked back over at Eric, who was now standing up to stretch, she saw someone enter the room behind Eric and then immediately lunge for him.

Summer dropped her paintbrush and her canvas fell, banging into the paint table, and spilling paint all over Eric and the intruder. Or were they the intruders? Had Eric lied to her? Had they totally just been busted for breaking and entering and painting? Was that even a real crime?

Then as the commotion subsided Summer saw that the intruder was Seth. His face now covered in blue paint.

"Cohen?!" she exclaimed. "What are you doing here?"

"Your stepmom told me you were out in Laguna. I wanted to apologize. And then I thought he was posing nude for you."

"For what?" Summer asked, getting pissed as she tried to help Eric up from the mess.

"For stalking you yesterday," he said meekly.

"And what do you think you're doing now?" Summer asked, her hands on her hips.

"Apologizing," Seth squeezed out softly, backing away from Summer, who was just about ready to hit him.

"Cohen. Seriously. What is wrong with you? Why are you doing this? I'm on vacation and having fun." She pointed to Eric. "Meeting new people. Even learning some new things. So butt out," she ended with a scream. "Before my rage blackouts come back," she shouted as she wielded a paintbrush in her hand.

And Seth shyly disappeared out the door. Humiliated. Summer felt bad for him for just a second, until she saw how covered in paint Eric was.

"Are you okay?" she asked.

"Yeah," he said. "Just a little messy."

"Umm . . ." she started as she looked at Eric. "How are we going to get back? You can't ride back in the car like that. I'll get you a towel. You can ride back in that."

"It's okay. I'll take the bus. I would hate to see what would happen if he came back and actually found me naked. Call me if you guys work things out," Eric said as he walked out the door, leaving Summer all alone.

On her way out, Summer looked at Eric's canvas and found that he had been painting a portrait of her. It was completely destroyed and covered with splattered paint, but she could tell it was very Picasso-esque, and very much her.

17

"Why are you so blue?" Ryan laughed as he found Seth in the kitchen trying to scrub the blue paint off of his face.

"I'm a stalker," Seth muttered over the running water.

"I've heard of masks. Ski caps. Stockings. But the Blue Man Group? That's a pretty good cover," Ryan said as he poured himself a glass of milk.

"Funny," Seth said, looking up from the sink. His face was dripping blue. "You were right. I went and saw her, and she called me a stalker."

"Hate to say it," Ryan said as he took a sip of his drink and sat at the table, reading the latest issue of the Young Avengers.

"But 'I told you so.' I know," Seth began. "But, Ryan, you don't understand. The guy was like teaching her to paint."

"Hands-around-the-back, *Ghost*-style kind of paint?" Ryan asked.

"No. They were sitting next to each other. But he was going to pose nude for her."

"Really?" Ryan asked, choking on his drink.

Seth shook his head. "No. I thought he was and that's why I flipped out and tackled him."

"Good move. Looks like it worked out well for you," Ryan said, paging through the comic book.

"Thanks," Seth said and went back to scrubbing his face. Ryan continued to read and sip his milk. By the time Seth had finished removing the blue from his skin, he was completely defeated, and his face was red and raw from all the scrubbing. "This sucks," Seth said as he sat down next to Ryan. "What am I supposed to do now?"

But Ryan had no answer. Seth had crossed the line of crazy.

18

What am I supposed to do now? Summer wondered. Seth was a stalker. Eric probably never wanted to get near her again. And she had forged some sort of secret bond with the monster. Had her vacation gone from being a disaster to being just fine to becoming a disaster again?

Summer sat alone in her suite icing the bruise on her thumb—a semipermanent reminder of Eric. Of her day spent building a house. And her first day spent being spied on because she knew that was why Ryan had shown up—Seth had persuaded him. Somehow. *Why did Cohen always have to meddle in her business?*

She really liked Eric. And even though she was looking forward to their first kiss, she wasn't even sure her feelings were romantic ones. For the most part, she was happy to have a friend who was a guy. A friend with a different perspective who opened her up to a whole new world, and she liked that she was doing well at his challenges so far.

Even if she ended up with a bruised thumb and paint in her hair.

But now, because of Cohen, she was sitting all alone in her suite. *When would all the drama end?* She wasn't about to call Cohen and apologize or even try to sort things out. That wasn't why she was on vacation. And she didn't really want to give him that kind of satisfaction. That's what he wanted from her. If she called him and tried to explain or apologize, then that gave him a sliver, a slight opening in the door, and then he would feel like he owned her again. That she was all his.

And she wasn't. Not now. Especially not now.

What she *really* needed to figure out was what she would say to Eric. How she would explain herself to him. How she could get him back in her life.

Would she just walk up to him and tell him sorry for having an ex-boyfriend who was so psycho? Or would she need something bigger? He was, after all, the kind of guy who knew everything and everyone in Laguna. He was more worldly. More experienced.

She needed a plan. Something to . . .

But her thoughts were interrupted by a knock at the door. Summer opened it to find her dad standing there. She looked past him, expecting to see the monster, but she wasn't there. It was just her dad.

"I came to say thanks," he said as he entered her room.

"For what?" Summer asked, curious.

"She said you were great this morning."

Then Summer remembered helping her stepmom find her wedding ring and realized that's what her dad was talking about.

Summer told her dad it was nothing, then slumped onto her bed.

"I know this wasn't your dream vacation, but why so down?" he asked.

"Remember Seth?" she asked.

"The Iceman with the vim and the vigor?"

Summer nodded.

Sitting down next to her on the bed, he said, "I thought you guys were over."

"We were. I mean we'll always be friends, but now with Eric . . ."

"Who's Eric?" he asked.

"The boy I was with today."

"And you like this Eric guy?"

"Yes. No." Summer thought about it for a second. Did she really like Eric? Or was she more in awe of the fact that he wasn't Cohen? That his view of the world—of life—was different? "I don't know. He's different."

Her dad nodded and thought about what Summer had said. She knew he was formulating some great response. A fabulous piece of advice. That's what he always did. At least what he used to do when they were really close. Lately, she'd felt them drifting apart. She wasn't sure whether it was the monster's fault or her own. If she was the one who was too busy with school and her friends and

Zach and Seth and whatever other drama was going on her life or if he had become too wrapped up in work and taking care of the monster.

"I miss this," Summer finally blurted out, thinking about the times when the two of them used to sit up late at night and talk.

Her dad nodded in agreement.

"I've got an idea," he said. "How about tomorrow, we spend the day together? Like we used to."

"What about—" Summer tried to ask, remembering that the monster didn't do so well on her own.

"I'll get her a whole day at the spa. It'll be fine. And fun. Now get some rest," her dad said as he kissed her on the forehead, like he used to when she was a kid.

"Good night," she whispered as he opened the door to exit.

Good night, he winked back at her. Summer lay on the bed and thought about the day, about the men in her life, and was glad to have her dad back. Even if it was only for a day.

After a night filled with jumbled thoughts and emotions masquerading as dreams and nightmares, Summer awoke to her dad knocking at her door. "Wake up," he called. She groggily got out of bed and let him in.

"What time is it?" she asked, brushing her tousled hair out of her eyes.

"Ten. Get dressed. We've got a big day ahead of us," he said with a giant smile.

Summer could taste the night on her breath. She needed a toothbrush bad. "Give me fifteen minutes," she said as she retreated to her bathroom.

"I'll meet you in the lobby," he said, leaving her to get ready.

"Okay," she called out before the door shut behind him.

While she was in the shower, Summer thought about the day ahead of her. She wondered what her dad had planned. If they were just going to lie by the pool all day? Or if he had thought of something better, more entertaining? Then Summer caught herself. Had Eric rubbed off on her? Had she really just wished for something more to do than lie by the pool all day?

She quickly washed her face and put on a light coat of makeup. Then threw on her bathing suit, a top, and a skirt. She took one quick glance in the mirror and was out the door. She didn't bother to give herself a complete once-over in the mirror, like she normally did before going out in public. It just didn't seem important.

Summer found her dad in the lobby of the hotel, talking to someone in the chair across from him. She figured he had just run into one of his business associates, but when she rounded the corner and could finally see the guy's face, she realized it was Eric.

Her insides flopped.

"Hey, look who I found?" her dad said when he saw her approaching. Summer gave Eric a nod. She wasn't sure how to respond. "Eric was just telling me all that you guys have been up to over the past couple days. Sounds pretty exciting."

Summer smiled. It was. But what else had Eric told her father and since when did guys she liked just approach her dad and tell him what they were thinking? Feeling. Let alone what they'd been doing with his daughter.

And did this mean that Eric had forgiven her for yesterday's debacle?

"I guess I'll leave you two alone. Have fun today," Eric said to her, then gave her a friendly hug. *I guess he's not mad,* she thought as Eric let go and said good-bye to her dad.

"Where to?" Summer turned and asked her dad once Eric was out of sight.

"How about the beach?" he suggested.

"Sure," Summer replied unenthusiastically. She didn't really want to spend the day lying in the sun, but she didn't want to say no to her dad. It was her one and only chance this vacation to have him all to herself and she didn't want to ruin the opportunity.

The sun was high overhead by the time they reached the beach. Summer pulled her towel out of her bag and unfolded it in the wind, but as it settled onto the sand and she prepared to take a seat, her dad stopped her.

"What do you think you're doing?" he asked.

"Laying out. The thing I do when I go to the beach," Summer replied matter-of-factly.

"Maybe that's what you do now, with Marissa. But what about the old Summer?" Summer looked at her dad. What was he talking about? "The Summer who wanted to be a mermaid. The Summer who spent her summers collecting shells and telling stories."

"I was eight," Summer said. She wanted to spend time with her dad, but it appeared he was going crazy. As she sat down on her towel, Summer wondered if her stepmother's problems could be contagious.

Her dad stood, looking down at her. "I miss those days," her dad said.

And Summer understood. He wanted to go back to the days when she was eight. She dug her hand in the sand next to her and let the sand slip through her fingers until the only thing left in her palm was a tiny seashell. She turned back to her dad and held it out for him to see.

"This," she began, "is one lonely shell."

Her dad sat down next to her, then took the shell from her hand and placed it in his own. "Let's call him Eric."

"Really?" Summer asked. The image of Eric popped into her head.

"Yeah. Why not?"

Summer shrugged her shoulders. "No reason," she covered, even though they both knew the reason why.

"He's lonely because he's miles away from home," her dad began.

"And has no friends here," Summer added.

"He keeps trying to make friends. But he's so different. See that brown stripe right there?" Her dad held out the shell and pointed to a little mark on it. "Keeps everyone away."

"But one day," Summer started as she sifted her hands through the sand again and came up with another shell. "He met this great big beautiful shell." She held it up next to her dad's hand.

"And they started talking. And realized that even though they'd spent their lives living miles apart from each other they had a lot in common," her dad added as he placed his shell into Summer's palm, alongside the other.

"So they became friends."

"And they lived happily ever after," her father ended.

Summer stood up from her towel and walked down to the water, where she stood looking at the dozens of sailboats out at sea. She thought about Seth. Then she looked in her hand and saw the two shells, happily sitting next to each other. And with one giant throw, she tossed the two shells into the water, back to their home. And she wondered about Eric. What would happen with them?

Her dad approached with a laugh. "You always sent them back home, didn't you?"

Summer turned away from the waves and looked at her dad with a grin. He knew her too well. And that's why she loved him.

"Let's take a walk," her dad suggested. "See what else we can find."

Summer nodded. And they began walking down the beach, away from the resort.

After they had walked for twenty minutes or so, they came to a small outcropping of rock. Summer climbed up on top of one and took a seat. Her dad followed and sat down next to her.

"So, Eric seems nice."

Summer nodded. "Yeah. He is."

"I like him," he said.

Me, too, Summer wanted to say, but she didn't. She couldn't. She was afraid. Whenever her dad liked someone she was remotely interested in, it meant that it was going to get serious. But all she really wanted from Eric was a kiss. One small kiss. Something to make this vacation exciting. But now that her dad had already approved of Eric, it seemed different. What had happened to the fun? His challenges to her? She just wanted to prove that she wasn't shallow or superficial. And she wanted a kiss as a reward.

"Summer?" her dad said, snapping her out of her train of thought.

Summer shook her head and looked at him. "Sorry." She bent down and picked up a shell. "This is Adam."

"Adam, huh? I don't think so," he said and picked the shell out of her hand. He held it between his fingers for a second, then tossed it into the water.

"Hey," she said as she watched the shell sink into the blue waves.

"I can tell there's something on your mind and I don't think it's Adam. I had to let him go, so you could talk. What is it?"

Summer wished she had a concrete answer but she didn't. Now that the entire Eric-and-Seth drama had surfaced, this vacation was starting to seem even worse. She didn't know what she wanted.

"I don't know," Summer said, knowing that her dad would eventually pull it out of her. He was good like that.

"Let's see. You stopped talking and went into your Summerland place when I mentioned Eric. Does he have something to do with it?"

Summer nodded yes.

"And I'm guessing Seth probably has something to do with it, too?"

Summer smiled a half smile.

"So, boy trouble. Makes sense. You're a beautiful young lady."

"Dad," Summer said bashfully.

"I can say nice things about my only daughter."

Summer laughed.

"So, they're fighting over you?"

"No. Yes. Sort of."

"But you like them both," he stated.

"For different reasons," Summer admitted.

"And those would be?"

Summer picked up another shell and tossed it into the water. Then she thought about both the boys. Seth was her ex, her friend, sort of everything to her in terms of guys. And Eric, well, he was new and adventurous and brought out the better things in her. But how could she explain this to her dad? "I don't know. They're both good friends."

"There's nothing wrong with having guys as friends," her dad said. This struck a chord with Summer. She'd never really made a conscious effort to make a guy friend and her dad was right, there was nothing wrong with having guys as friends. She always had ulterior motives. She always wanted the kiss. The relationship. More. But her dad was right, why couldn't Eric and Seth just be her friends?

"Thanks," she said, then picked up another shell. "This is Amanda." And she held it out for her dad to look.

"Who never ceases to amaze me," her dad said as he picked up the shell and looked at Summer, speaking more to her than the shell.

Summer's dimples brightened her cheeks. "And always has someone to fall back on when she's got a problem." She looked back at her father, who now held the shell tight in his hands.

"And knows that the best place to find love is home." Then he tossed the shell back into the water and stood up.

As Summer and her dad made their way back through the resort and up to the suites, Summer thought about her dad's advice. They could just be friends. She and Eric *and* she and Seth. Now all she had to do was explain to Seth that being friends meant not stalking each other. But she figured that could wait until tomorrow. Today would just be for family and she would have dinner with her dad and stepmom and tomorrow she would call Seth and-explain the situation to him. Then she would find Eric and tell him that she'd sorted things out with Seth. And then *maybe* she could get that kiss—she stopped herself. *Old habits really do die hard,* she thought as she imagined kissing Eric. She was supposed to be his friend. Maybe she could allow herself just one slipup. No one ever succeeded when they quit cold turkey.

But as she and her dad approached the pool area, Summer saw Seth coming down the stairs from the main lobby. *Great.* Maybe she would have to have the no-stalking talk much sooner than expected. So much for a day full of family.

Summer tried to turn the other way and run and hide, but Seth saw her and came running down the stairs.

"Wait." He put out his hand. "Please. Just let me apologize."

Summer looked at her dad, who took a step back and allowed them to continue.

"You have one minute," Summer said, holding up one finger for emphasis.

"I'm sorry I ditched you. I'm sorry I sent Ryan to spy on you. I'm sorry for everything," Seth babbled.

"What about the stalking?"

"What stalking?" Seth tried to cover.

"You're kidding me right?" Summer said in disbelief. And before they knew it, they were screaming at each other, all their frustrations coming out. Louder . . . and . . . louder . . .

Until her dad finally stepped in and stuck up for her.

"Maybe you should go home now, Seth."

Both of them were quiet for a second and looked at her dad. "You two can sort this out later when we get back to Newport," he told them.

With that, Seth left, and Summer left wondering if she really could be friends with a guy.

19

Ryan and Marissa were hanging out in the pool house playing PlayStation, when Seth came barging in.

"I stalked her," he blurted out.

"What's new?" Ryan asked, barely looking up from the game.

"Again. This time her dad was there. He told me to leave. It's so over."

"You went back?" Marissa asked as she put down her controller.

"We're playing here," Ryan said as he watched Marissa's car crash and burn on the screen. "You just died."

"Ryan, I'm dying here," Seth said as he flopped onto the bed.

"I told you not to go back there. Just let it sit."

"Thanks, buddy. Obviously I didn't take the advice," Seth sighed.

"Ryan," Marissa exclaimed. "Be a little nicer."

Ryan finally pressed PAUSE on the game and focused on Seth. "So now what?"

Seth looked to Marissa for an answer.

"Don't look at me. I already told you I wasn't getting involved," she said.

Seth gave her puppy-dog eyes. "Please."

Ryan looked at Marissa. "Help him, otherwise he's going to be this pathetic until she gets back," Ryan begged.

Marissa thought for a minute. She didn't want to sell out her friend again, but maybe there was something she could do. "I may have an idea."

Seth sat at attention and got really excited.

"No more stalking," Ryan said, shooting Seth down just an inch.

"No. Tomorrow I have to help my mom with this fashion show. I'll enlist Summer's help. Then you guys can come and you can make up."

"Brilliant. Me in my own environment. It's perfect. I can't fail." Seth's face brightened.

Ryan gave him his brooding look.

"Okay, maybe I can," Seth admitted. "But it's worth a shot." Seth gave Marissa a giant hug. "I think I might love you."

"Don't go there, Cohen. I don't need a stalker," Marissa joked.

"Funny. Ryan, did you know Marissa was so funny?"

"Actually? Yeah. I did," Ryan said as the three friends went back to playing PlayStation. Wasting time until tomorrow.

20

That night Summer actually had an enjoyable dinner with her family. The stepmonster was unusually nice and Summer and her dad forged a new bond.

After Summer said good night to both of them she decided that she would take her father's advice and go see Eric. She couldn't wait until tomorrow. She had to apologize for all of the Seth drama and she missed her new friend.

Summer had spent at least half an hour going from Eric's villa to the pool, to the restaurant, to the ballroom, even to the beach, but only after she'd exhausted all the possibilities did she remember that Eric's quiet place was the garden.

She found him standing in the butterfly garden.

Summer approached, then whispered, "Hey."

A bit startled, Eric spun around to find her standing there. "I'm sorry," she said, before he even had a chance to acknowledge her presence. But Eric just shook his head. Summer realized she'd have to do better. "I'm sorry for Cohen. But he's

Cohen and I just didn't know . . ." Eric still said nothing, his head moving back and forth. This wasn't working. Summer started again, "I really am sor—"

But Eric cut her off before she could say anything else. "You ever hear of American Steel?"

Summer shook her head. What was he talking about?

"I didn't think so," he said, then shook *his* head.

"I'm sorry," Summer started. *How many times do I have to say those words?* "I don't know it. I wish I did. But I'm being honest. I don't know what you're talking about."

"I know," he said again, shaking his head. "My dad owns it."

"And I'm sor—"

"Don't say it," he said as he put a finger to her lips.

"But I'm s—" she tried again, only to be silenced once more.

"I'm sorry," he finally said.

"For what?" Summer asked, now totally thrown off guard.

"For yesterday. For leaving you with that crazy guy."

"Cohen," Summer said, filling in the blanks.

Eric nodded. "Yeah. But that's not why I left."

"Then why?" Summer asked. She took a step closer to him, then sat on the cool evening grass. Eric sat down next to her.

"I was just frustrated with myself. Lying to you, trying to play someone I wasn't."

"What are you talking about?" Summer asked, now utterly confused.

"Me. The fact that my bedroom window overlooks Lake Michigan. That there are two floors to our penthouse suite."

"You live in a penthouse? That's so cool," Summer said, now more into Eric than ever. He was her friend, but now that she knew this, that longing for a kiss was starting to return.

"Exactly what I thought you'd say," he said as he lay back in the grass and looked up at the stars. "What everyone always says."

Summer lay back as well; she could feel the summer heat escaping the ground. And she wondered what was going through Eric's head. Why did he care what everyone always said?

"Isn't living in a penthouse a good thing?" she finally asked.

"Sure," he said after a moment's hesitation. "If that's all you ever want people to know about you."

"But there's so much more. You're like Mister Laguna. You've been everywhere. Know everyone," Summer said as she reflected back on the past few days that they had hung out together. On all the things he had shown her, taught her.

"What if I had told you all this when I had first met you?" Eric asked.

"I would have become your friend much quicker," Summer said with a smile.

"Exactly. And exactly not what I wanted."

"What's that?" Summer asked, a little offended. Why didn't he want to be her friend?

"You don't get it, do you?"

Summer shook her head no. He was talking in circles now and she was totally clueless.

"If I had told you all this, you wouldn't have seen me as the guy from the, what do you call it?"

"The flyover zone," Summer said.

"That's it."

"Well, I think you're much more than that," she said.

"Thanks," he said, smiling at her for the first time that night. Summer could almost feel his breath upon her cheek. Her body rushed with that-tingling sensation you get right before you kiss-someone. She inched her head a little closer to-his.

"You're welcome," she responded, then moved a little closer. This was it. This was the moment she had been waiting for the past week. The first kiss. She leaned in closer to him. His breath warm on her cheek. The tingles rushing through her veins. Then she closed her eyes and moved even closer. Then she waited . . .

But there was no kiss.

Just Eric backing away from her.

"I thought we were friends," Eric said as he sat up.

"We are," Summer said, taken aback.

"Then what . . ."

Summer just shrugged it off. "Never mind. I'm

glad I did all this for nothing," she said as she looked at the blisters on her hands and the bruised thumb.

"You didn't do it for nothing," he tried to explain.

But Summer didn't want to hear it. She was already humiliated. She'd tried to kiss Eric and he'd turned her down.

She stood and started to walk away.

"It's okay," she explained. "I get it." *You're just not into me.* The thought jarred her. This was a first. But she guessed this vacation was turning out to be a complete trip of firsts. First time making tortillas, first time building a house, first time painting, first time being stalked, and first time being completely rejected by a guy.

Summer turned her walk into a run as she headed back to her suite. She didn't really want to talk to Eric and she barely made out the words as he yelled after her, "It wasn't for nothing."

When Summer made it back to her room, she took a hot shower and tried to wash away the humiliation and embarrassment. Why had she tried to kiss him? Why couldn't she have just taken her father's advice and kept Eric as a friend?

But what was done was done, she thought and there was no turning back.

As she got out of the shower and readied for bed, she thought about Eric and the week and his cryptic conversation about his penthouse and how he wanted people to see him for who he really was.

Then she wondered if that was what Eric was trying to do to her. Force her to see herself for who she really was. She had learned a lot about herself over the past week and now as she thought about it maybe it hadn't been for nothing. She knew now that tortillas were made of a lot of grease, and that she was a horrible painter and not so good with building. But she was okay with all this.

Eric had made her realize that she didn't want to change. That she liked the Summer Roberts that she was. Even if she did come across as superficial and shallow. At least now she knew that there was a world out there beyond her Newport Beach bubble. But it didn't mean she had to go live there.

THE OC

21

"Rise and shine, Ryan. It's a beautiful day in the neighborhood," Seth said as he entered the pool house and began opening all the blinds.

"Okay, Mr. Rogers. What time is it?" Ryan asked, barely turning over and trying to shield his eyes from the blinding sun pouring through his windows.

"Seven A.M. sharp," Seth replied with enthusiasm.

"And why are we up this early?" Ryan asked, pulling the blankets back over his head.

"Dude. It's redemption day. Seth Cohen reborn . . . renewed." Seth pulled the covers off of Ryan's head.

"I don't think it's the same thing," Ryan muttered, pulling the blankets back up.

"With the help of your lovely little Marissa, I am going to redeem myself with Summer. We will be friends at last. Even if I have to tie her down and—"

"It's too early to start stalker talk," Ryan whispered from under the covers.

Seth finally pounced on the bed and pulled all the covers off Ryan.

"Don't tell me you have another ingenious plan that ends in stalking or making some grand gesture," Ryan said.

"No plans. Just good old friendship," Seth said as he happily went around the room tidying things up. Pulling clothes out of the closet for Ryan and tossing them on the bed. "See you at breakfast. We'll talk then."

Great, Ryan thought, knowing this couldn't end well, but hoping it would.

22

Summer awoke with a new sense of purpose. She was an O.C. girl through and through. Born and raised in Newport Beach, California, and she was proud of it.

Now, all she had to do was tell Eric. Apologize for not understanding what he was talking about the previous night. Apologize for not thanking him for all that he'd shown her. But most of all apologize for trying to kiss him. She got it now. She understood what it meant to have a guy just be a friend. And she wanted Eric to be that friend.

Summer dressed in her favorite bikini and Juicy Couture hoodie and skirt and went to find Eric. She was on a mission.

After searching all over the resort, Summer finally found Eric at the least likely spot, his villa.

She knocked on the door and his stepmom, who was surprisingly cordial, let her in. She wasn't anything like the stepmonster and Summer wondered what she had done to Eric to make him hate her so much, but she let it slide. When she knocked on Eric's door, her hands started to get clammy.

Why was she nervous? He was only a friend. Nothing more. Then she remembered her awful attempt to kiss him. Her face reddened. But she took a deep breath. She could hear his footsteps getting closer to the door. She wiped her palms on her skirt and told herself to relax. It was just one embarrassing moment and she was on a mission.

The door opened and Eric stood staring at her, wearing nothing but his khaki shorts.

She took another deep breath. *Being friends is hard when a guy's got muscles like that.*

"Just give me one minute," Summer said. She put her hand on the door to stop him from shutting it.

Eric took a step back and let her into the room.

"I'm not going to say the word *sorry,*" Summer began. "But I just want you to know that I get it."

Eric nodded and sat on his bed, obviously waiting for more.

"And," Summer started again. "I think you should know that I am happy being Summer Roberts. The cooking, the art, the building? All great things and it's good to know there's another world out there. But I think I like my little home here in Southern California."

Eric nodded again. Waiting.

Summer took another deep breath. *He wanted*

more? "Okay. I may come off as superficial and shallow, but I'm okay with it. I don't need to prove myself otherwise, 'cause I know, my friends know, and well, I hope you—" She couldn't finish her sentence. "And I get it. If you don't want to be friends with a spoiled O.C. girl, that's okay. I just wanted to say thanks." And with that, Summer turned and began to walk out the door. That was the first honest conversation she'd had with a boy in a long time, if not ever.

"Wait," Eric called out.

Summer turned around and looked at him.

"Want to go to the pool?" he asked. And in that moment, she knew, she had a friend for life.

Summer nodded. She liked that he said everything with just one question. One invite. She didn't want to wax poetic or talk philosophy on friendships. She just wanted him to know that she was grateful for what he had done and she wanted him to know that they could be friends.

And he'd accepted.

At the pool, Summer let Eric convince her to forego the lying out and actually get in the water and play. Summer had reluctantly agreed on the account that this would be the last "lesson in the ways of Eric," as she had called it.

Eric had agreed to her request and then promptly pushed her into the water with a big splash. When Summer came up for air, she immediately grabbed Eric's shoulders and tried to dunk him. The two splashed around like two little kids on too much candy.

They had so much fun that the entire kids' camp decided to join them. Everyone played Marco Polo and other kid games in the water, until Summer's fingers started to prune and she could feel the skin on her face tightening from too much chlorine.

"I'm going to take a break," Summer explained to Eric and the kids as she got out of the water. All the kids booed, but Summer just had to get out. At least for fifteen minutes or so.

But as she exited the pool, she noticed Marissa walking toward her. Summer waved at her friend, but then she felt her stomach tighten. Was this another Cohen-esque disaster?

"Please tell me that you weren't sent here by Seth Cohen," Summer said as she grabbed a towel and greeted Marissa.

"Good to see you, too," Marissa answered. "And no, Seth did not send me."

Summer dried herself off and sat on one of the lounge chairs. Marissa sat across from her and took in the surroundings.

"Is that him?" Marissa asked as she gazed over at the pool.

Summer followed Marissa's gaze. "Yeah," she said, noticing that Eric was still in the pool playing with the kids.

"He's hot. No wonder Cohen's jealous," Marissa said as she stared at Eric and his swimmer's body.

Summer looked at her friend. "He sent you, didn't he?"

Marissa started to stammer and hesitate, but she couldn't hide this from her best friend. "Okay, he did. But only sort of."

"How sort of?" Summer asked as she looked over at the bushes just waiting for Cohen to pop out of them at any minute.

"After his last disaster he came home and I was hanging out with Ryan. He roped me into it."

"What does he want now? Are you supposed to tie me up and bring me back to him?"

"No. Of course not. Here's the 'sort of' part. I need your help. I was going to come here anyways, then Cohen found out I was going and he's really hard to say no to."

"I know," Summer said, remembering how he had pursued her in the first place, professing his love for her.

"My mom's doing this kids' fashion show thing and I can't do it alone. She's making me help her and I volunteered you, too. I thought you might need a little Newport society love."

Summer laughed. "I'll do it. On one condition," she began as she reflected on her week here at Seascape with Eric. It was her turn to teach him a thing or two. "Eric comes with."

Marissa hesitated. "You know Cohen and Ryan will be there?"

Summer nodded, *so*? She didn't care anymore.

"Eric's my friend. Cohen's my friend. I think it's time we all became friends."

Marissa said okay, then told Summer that she would get her car out of valet while Summer got Eric out of the pool.

Summer put on her cover-up and started getting ready. Eric noticed her dressing.

"Hey, where you going?" he shouted.

"It's a surprise," Summer said.

"I like surprises," he yelled back as he made his way to the ladder and fought his way through a pack of kids who didn't want to let him go. "My princess calls," he told them as he got out of the water and walked over to Summer, who was waiting with a towel.

"Funny," Summer said as she handed him his towel.

"What are we doing?" he asked, putting on his shirt.

"It's time to meet the real Summer Roberts," Summer said with a smile.

"I thought we went over this. We're friends."

"Just trust me," she said, recalling all the times he'd convinced her to do something new just by saying the words *trust me.*

"Ow. Touché," he said, following Summer toward the main entrance where Marissa was waiting with her car.

"So this is the lovely Marissa," he said with a smile as he gently shook her hand.

"Yes. Now stop the flirting," Summer said as she got into the car. "And get in. It's time for me to educate you."

"To Newport," Marissa shouted.

"Home," Summer said as she turned around and smiled at Eric.

23

The first stop on the road back home was Fashion Island. Marissa pulled up to the valet and they got out of the car.

"That's Neiman's," Summer said as she pointed out the large department store and grabbed Eric's hand to lead him closer. "It's Marissa's favorite."

Eric looked back at Marissa as if to check Summer's statement. Marissa smiled.

Summer was right. Marissa loved Neiman's. It was her escape. Her hideaway when Newport became too much to handle.

"Hey, Coop," Summer yelled back to her friend. "Where we going?"

"Hold on," Marissa said as she pulled out a piece of paper from her back pocket. Her mom had given her a list of stores that were loaning their clothes for the fashion show. Marissa started reading, "Cassie's boutique. BCBG. Chanel. Gucci. And I think that shoe store that has all the Jimmy Choos and Manolo Blahniks." Marissa finished and caught up with Summer and Eric.

The threesome stood in the middle of Fashion Island. The water of the fountain splashing behind them and the sun of California beating down on them. Summer took a deep breath.

"It feels good to be back," she said, then turned to Eric. "Isn't this great?"

Eric just shook his head as he watched several young girls walk by carrying Hermes bags and talking on their cell phones.

"Oh, no," Summer said. She reached out and put her hand on Eric's cheek, stilling his head. "There's none of that. You said you trusted me. That was the deal. This is my challenge to you. Make it through today and maybe we'll keep in touch."

"A challenge, huh?" Eric asked hesitantly as overly dressed-up girls walked by him. Summer nodded and Eric couldn't resist. "I'm in."

"First stop?" Marissa said as she walked out in front of Summer and Eric to say that she was the leader. "Cassie's."

Summer grabbed Eric's hand again and the two followed Marissa through the outdoor mall. Summer felt his strong grip against the inside of her palm and for the first time since she had met Eric, she felt calm and in her element. She liked this new sense of control. Now that they'd agreed to just be friends, Summer felt relaxed around him, like she didn't have to prove herself anymore. That she could just be Summer. And she liked it.

When they reached Cassie's, Marissa went to the cashier and found the manager, who directed the three of them to a back storage closet.

"Wow," Eric said as he saw the shopping bags filled with clothes. "Is that all for you guys?"

"That's just the beginning," Marissa giggled and looked over at Summer, who was going through the clothes.

"I wish I was still this size," Summer said as she held a dress against her front, imagining what it would be like to be ten again.

"Aren't you?" Eric asked.

"Isn't he sweet?" Summer said as she took Eric's compliment. "So is this for Kaitlin?" Summer asked, remembering that Marissa's sister was back from boarding school.

"No," Marissa said. "It's some event my mom wanted to do to raise money for some charity. But let's be honest, you know she's just trying to shape all of Newport's youth into the next Julie Cooper."

Summer couldn't stop laughing. But when she looked at Eric she could see that he didn't get it, so she stopped herself and explained, "Marissa's mom is sort of the queen of Newport's social scene in the adult world. Marissa is the queen of our world."

"I'm not the queen of anything," Marissa added as she picked up a couple of bags and gestured for Eric to pick up the rest.

"Marissa's a rebel," Summer said with a smirk.

Eric laughed. "I can see that."

"Hey," Marissa said as they made their way out of the store. "I take offense at that." Marissa giggled then, changed her mind. "Actually, rebel's hot. I like you," she finished to Eric.

Summer gave Eric a pat on the back as Marissa started to lead them through the mall again. "Told you this wouldn't be so bad."

"You were right," Eric started, then looked down at the giant bags he was carrying. "And I even get a workout."

"Hang out with me, you never know what you'll learn," Summer said as they followed after Marissa.

After a whirlwind few hours of shopping, it was finally time for the actual event. Eric helped the girls unload Marissa's car and bring the clothes into the ballroom of the Four Seasons.

"Summer, you made it," Julie said. "And I see you brought a friend."

"Oh, sorry," Summer said when she realized that Eric was standing quietly next to her. "Mrs. Cooper, this is Eric. We met at Seascape. He spends his summers there."

"Great. Good. What I really need is someone to help me move all these tables," Julie said as she grabbed Eric and pulled him over to ballroom. "The water polo team backed out on me."

"Bye," Summer whispered with a smirk as Eric disappeared with Julie Cooper. *He'll definitely learn something now.*

Backstage, there were about twenty girls under ten running around getting ready. Marissa and Summer had been put in charge of wrangling the girls and making sure they were ready to go when the lights when down.

"So," Marissa began. "You and Eric?"

"Friends," Summer replied.

"Really?" Marissa asked. A little blond approached her and held out her dress choice. Marissa shook her head no and sent the girl back to the racks. "But he's so—"

"Cute. I know."

"And nothing ever happened?"

"Nothing," Summer said, remembering how she had tried to kiss him, how she had waited all week for the moment. But now she was glad nothing had happened. She wondered how well he was doing moving tables for Mrs. Cooper.

"I'm impressed," Marissa said. The little blond returned and this time Marissa approved of the dress.

"What about you? Any new men while I was gone?"

Marissa shook her head, then directed another girl back to the racks.

"That's okay," Summer said. "We still have the rest of the summer, you know?"

"And there's always Seth and Ryan," Marissa added.

"True. But do we really want to try that again?"

Marissa shrugged her shoulders. "Who knows?"

"Yeah. Wait. Speaking of the boys, weren't they supposed to be here?"

Then Marissa remembered as well. "Oh, no. They were and they're probably . . ." Her voice trailed off as she hurried toward the ballroom. Summer followed close behind.

Marissa stopped short as they came to the ballroom doors. When she opened them, there they were. Julie Cooper with Eric, and Ryan and Cohen approaching the pair. A complete disaster waiting to happen.

Summer had to stop them. She ran into the ballroom and grabbed Eric's hand, then quickly ushered him backstage to an area where all the girls were putting on makeup.

"What was that all about?"

"Nothing. I just—" Summer looked around for-an excuse. "I needed your help with—" She picked up a compact full of eye shadows. A kaleidoscope of colors. "With this makeup. Too many girls here. I can't do it all myself."

"Um, Summer," he started as he looked at the vanity table full of makeup he'd never seen before, let alone knew what to do with. "In case you forgot, I'm a guy."

"I know that," Summer covered quickly. She needed an excuse. Something else. She didn't want to deal with Cohen and Eric meeting yet. Then she remembered their day at the art gallery. "It's just like painting," she explained. "Only, it's living art." Summer looked to Eric. Had he bought it?

Eric hesitated, then . . .

One of the little blonds approached them as they both sat at the vanity. "Is he going to do my makeup?" the little girl asked.

"Yes. As a matter of fact, he is," Summer said.

Summer handed Eric a brush and a palette of color. "Living art," she told him as she walked away. Eric reluctantly took the brush and began to carefully put eye shadow on the blond girl.

Summer sat back and watched how gentle and funny Eric was as he applied the makeup to the girl. The two of them really started enjoying their time together.

When Eric finished with the blond, he turned her seat around and showed her the mirror. "I look so pretty," the little girl said. Then she turned to Summer. "You have a nice boyfriend."

Summer looked at the girl, then explained, "He's not my boyfriend, just a really good friend." Summer looked over at Eric, who was now fumbling with a tube of lipstick. "And sometimes those are better than boyfriends."

The little girl scurried off, leaving Summer and Eric alone.

"So how was Mrs. Cooper?" Summer asked, curious.

"Interesting. Never met a woman like her before," Eric said with a smile. "But that's not saying much," he finished as he took Summer's hand and gave it a friendly squeeze.

Summer looked into his eyes. *This friend thing is nice,* she thought, but then her thoughts were interrupted by a shout.

"I knew it!"

Summer turned around and saw Seth approaching. Eric scooted his chair away from Summer.

"It's you again," Seth said as he stood in front of the two of them.

"It's you again," Eric responded and stood up as if to leave.

"Don't go," Summer said and reached out for his hand.

"Summer, if he wants to leave he can. This is a free country," Seth said.

"No," Summer said, finally sticking up for herself, for her friends. "I want you two to meet. Formally. None of this stalker stuff."

Seth relented and Eric turned back.

"Eric, this is Seth. Seth, this is Eric. Now shake hands and be men."

"He's putting makeup on girls, how can we be—"

"Cohen!"

"Fine." Seth gave in and held out his hand. The two boys shook and Summer smiled. Two boys who were friends of hers could maybe finally get along. She'd help, but in the end it was up to them. And that was fine with her.

And Summer was happy.